D0889002

As
YOU
ARE

OTHER BOOKS AND AUDIO BOOKS

BY SARAH M. EDEN

Courting Miss Lancaster

The Kiss of a Stranger

Seeking Persephone

Friends and Foes

An Unlikely Match

Drops of Gold

Glimmer of Hope

As You Are

A Regency Romance

Sarah M. Eden

Covenant Communications, Inc.

Cover image: Photographer *Woman in Forest* © Susan Fox/Trevillion Images

Published by Covenant Communications, Inc.
American Fork, Utah

Printed in the United States of America
First Printing: January 2014

20 19 18 17 16 15 14   11 10 9 8 7 6 5 4 3

ISBN 978-1-62108-575-1

To Jonathan, my "Corbin,"
so quiet, so good and kind, and too often unaware of your worth.
Know that you are loved just exactly as you are.

Chapter One

April 1815
Nottinghamshire, England

Corbin Jonquil knew he really ought to be listening to the sermon. That was the point of attending church, after all. Of late, he seldom heard a single word the vicar uttered—not since Mrs. Bentford had joined the congregation. Mrs. Bentford, a widow of no more than twenty-two or twenty-three, possessing more than her share of beauty and a sizable enough portion to have purchased a more-than-respectable cottage nearby, had taken the neighborhood quite by storm only a few months earlier.

Rumors abounded regarding the latest addition to the very small circle of families surrounding the minuscule town of Grompton. Some claimed she had been married to a nabob with more fortune than status. Others believed she had possessed a fortune of her own and married a man beneath her for love. Nothing, however, raised greater speculation than her children.

Mrs. Bentford had two: a boy and a girl. Her son appeared to be six or seven years old and looked absolutely nothing like his mother. Her daughter appeared to be about three years old and her mother's exact copy in miniature. The neighborhood alternately labeled her son a stepchild, a product of her husband's first marriage, or a ward left to her by a distant relative. For a lady of twenty-two to have a seven-year-old son required her to have become a mother at the almost unmarriageable age of fifteen. Naturally, the neighborhood was agog with speculation.

Corbin's curiosity arose for entirely different reasons. Two months earlier, during an errand in Grompton, Mrs. Bentford had crossed his path.

Corbin had raised his hat as she'd passed. She had looked directly at him and smiled. In that brief moment, she had stolen his heart.

Corbin had sat behind Mrs. Bentford and her children every Sunday since, watching the young family and thinking of hundreds of things he might say to her. *Good morning. Good day. That is a lovely bonnet.* Inevitably, when services came to an end, Corbin watched her leave without uttering a single word.

He was watching her again. She didn't wear black or even gray, so her husband had, apparently, been gone for at least a year. That meant the little girl with hair the color of browned bread likely had hardly known her father. Corbin wondered if that was a tragedy or a blessing—he'd known fathers who fell under both categories.

The tiny Miss Bentford turned her head quickly, looking at Corbin out of the corner of her eye. The two of them played a game each Sunday. Corbin could not recall how it had begun, but he looked forward to it every week.

Little Miss Bentford looked at him again, not quite as quickly. Corbin smiled at her, and she turned her head forward once more. Three more times she looked back, and each time, Corbin managed to look surprised to find her looking at him.

The third time, the little girl began to giggle. Corbin laid his finger against his lips, reminding her to be quiet in church. She bit her lip and nodded, but her eyes danced with mirth. Corbin smiled, thoroughly pleased.

Mrs. Bentford bent toward her daughter, whispering something in her ear. The little girl smiled once more at Corbin, then turned to face the vicar. Mrs. Bentford, however, turned and, out of the corner of her eye, looked at Corbin.

He felt his breath catch. It was pathetic, really, being so aware of a lady who was entirely unaware of him. Being caught encouraging that lady's daughter to misbehave in church proved particularly embarrassing.

Corbin managed what he hoped was an apologetic smile. Mrs. Bentford quickly returned her gaze to the front, but Corbin thought, hoped, he saw a hint of a smile on her face as she turned.

What if she thinks I'm an idiot? Corbin had asked one of his brothers that question not a month earlier.

You're a Jonquil, Layton had answered. *Of course she'll think you're an idiot.*

Not the most encouraging brotherly advice.

He tried to think of something he might say to her. *I am sorry for encouraging your daughter to giggle.* No, that wouldn't do. *Your daughter is very pretty.* No. *You are very pretty.* Definitely not.

The services came to a close before Corbin managed to think of anything suitable. They had not been formally introduced, so the chance of having a conversation with her was remote at best. The entire neighborhood knew Mrs. Bentford kept to herself. Corbin did not even know if anyone among the worshipers could be counted on to offer an introduction.

Mrs. Bentford's daughter, it seemed, was unaware of the social conventions. She stood on the pew and turned to face Corbin. She whispered loudly enough for Corbin to easily hear her. "I saw you," she enthusiastically told him.

Corbin nodded, fighting down a blush. Why was it he colored like a schoolgirl whenever he was spoken to?

"We quiet," she added.

He nodded again.

"Alice," Mrs. Bentford interrupted the one-sided conversation. She turned those green eyes on Corbin, and he only barely managed to not stare. "I am sorry she has been disturbing you, sir."

She spoke to him. Mrs. Bentford actually spoke to him. She never had before.

"No, not . . . not at all," Corbin said, then felt like a complete imbecile for stumbling over a simple reply.

Mrs. Bentford smiled at him, much the same way she had that afternoon in Grompton. Any words that might have sprung to mind at that very opportune moment dissipated as he stood there, entranced.

"Good day," Mrs. Bentford offered, then took both of her children by the hand and made her way out of the church.

He'd missed the perfect opportunity. *Good day, Mrs. Bentford. How do you do?* He might have said any number of things. His brother Layton was apparently right: Jonquils were idiots.

Corbin nodded mutely to a few familiar faces as he stepped out of the Grompton chapel. His eyes immediately found Mrs. Bentford. A small group had gathered around and appeared to be peppering her with attempts at conversation. Her son clutched her hand as though it were his last remaining lifeline. Alice, her daughter, hovered nearby, not nearly as intimidated as her brother but with the same lack of enthusiasm over the gathering of strangers.

Not one of the Bentfords appeared pleased with the situation. *I should extricate them,* Corbin thought. He would probably make a spectacle of himself.

Mrs. Bentford attempted to work her way backward out of the crowd. They were closing ranks—she would never make it.

Corbin clutched his prayer book in his right hand. *Excuse me.* Maybe, *Pardon me.* After a fortifying breath, he stepped to the edge of the group. He smiled an apology before elbowing past the portly Mr. Chambers.

"Mrs. Bentford," Corbin managed to get out without hesitation or a stutter.

She turned her head and looked at him. There was no panic in her eyes but an air of calm. If her grip on her children hadn't been white-knuckled, Corbin might have thought she had no need of assistance.

You left this. No. *Did you leave this?* Corbin fluctuated a moment. But everyone was looking at him, expectantly. "I think we"—he paused long enough to execute a much-needed swallow—"have one another's prayer books."

He stood stiff and uncomfortable. A great many people watched him.

Mrs. Bentford looked confused for the briefest of moments before understanding settled in her eyes. "Might we step aside for a moment and remedy this mishap?" she suggested.

Corbin nodded. He probably should offer her his arm, but suddenly, it was all he could do to simply walk.

Mrs. Bentford offered a quick good day to those nearest her as she made her way through the group.

You seemed anxious to be away from the crowd. He'd never get that out whole. *The citizens of Grompton can be very curious.* She already knew that.

They reached the edge of the churchyard, far enough from the curious crowd for a modicum of comfort. Mrs. Bentford looked up at Corbin expectantly. She had green eyes. He'd noticed before, but they were still mesmerizing.

"The prayer books," she hinted.

"Oh, I, uh." Corbin stumbled over the words once more. "I didn't actually—" He stopped for a breath, frustrated with himself. He ought to have thought through this conversation more.

"I know it was a ruse, sir," Mrs. Bentford filled in his explanation. "One that, I assure you, is appreciated. But if we do not exchange books, the curious onlookers will realize the deception."

Corbin nodded. He held his prayer book out to her. She accepted it and gave him hers.

"We can—" *Switch them back next Sunday. Switch them back next Sunday.* "Switch them—around again next—later."

"The vicar and his wife are coming to Ivy Cottage for tea on Thursday at two o'clock," Mrs. Bentford said, her tone still quite calm and collected. "If you would like to come then, we could be properly introduced."

Corbin felt a touch of color rise in his cheeks. Social conventions dictated he should not have spoken to her until the appropriate introductions had been undertaken. He'd gone about this completely wrong. "Forgive me," he muttered.

"Your rescue was quite well executed," Mrs. Bentford said. "Thank you." She turned to her children. "Alice. Edmund."

Alice appeared to barely hold back a giggle. Edmund kept his head low and his hand desperately wrapped around his mother's.

"Good day," Mrs. Bentford said to Corbin.

All he managed was something that sounded horribly like a gurgle.

The moment Mrs. Bentford left the churchyard, Corbin slapped his hat against his thigh. He'd muddled it, just as he knew he would. He was no orator. He could seldom even form coherent sentences.

Thursday at two o'clock. Corbin repeated that to himself as he rode home to Havenworth. He had four days to rehearse a few sentences, to go through the most likely topics of conversation. Perhaps he could manage to not make an utter fool of himself . . . but he seriously doubted four days would be enough.

Chapter Two

"No, Alice," Clara said for what felt like the hundredth time in ten minutes.

"I want to stay," Alice said with an almighty pout.

"I am sorry, dearest." Clara spoke slowly to keep from snapping. "As I told you, you must take your nap while Mama's visitors have their tea."

"No nap," Alice said once again.

"Yes nap," Clara answered firmly.

"No." Alice nodded decisively.

Clara wished she could blame Alice's stubbornness on Mr. Bentford, but Clara was every bit as stubborn as he had been. She'd had to be.

"Suzie will have milk and cakes with you and Edmund before your nap," Clara said.

Alice pulled a face.

Clara took two long, deep breaths and attempted to regain her calm. She was not usually so short on patience.

The past few days had been trying. Why she had invited an unfamiliar gentleman to tea was absolutely beyond her. Since she did not even know the gentleman's identity—he hadn't written his name anywhere in his prayer book—there had been absolutely no way of canceling the invitation. She was at loose ends over it.

She took Alice's hand and led her up the stairs. Alice continued to declare her intention to stay but went willingly enough. Thank heavens the girl was tired. Alice could be difficult to physically subdue. She could throw a fit unmatched in nature when she chose.

Clara, still holding Alice by the hand, found Edmund precisely where she'd expected to find him: in a chair in his room with his nose in a book. The boy was forever reading. The only outdoor pursuit he had ever shown any interest in was horseback riding. Mr. Bentford had never been willing to part with the funds for a pony, and Clara certainly hadn't the funds now. They lived comfortably at Ivy Cottage and could continue to do so, but there was not enough for a pony or horse.

"It is time for a break, Edmund."

He nodded but didn't look up.

"You can read after tea, dear."

He nodded again, then reluctantly closed his book.

"Tea is in Alice's room today," Clara told Edmund, "so she can take her nap as soon as you have finished."

Edmund kept a finger in his book as he followed Clara into the room next to his. He would be reading again the moment Clara left. She would have to insist he and Alice spend the evening out of doors before dinner. Spring had come to Nottinghamshire, and with their coats on, the children wouldn't be too cold.

Suzie was just finishing setting out the children's tea when Clara led them inside Alice's room.

"Down," Alice demanded sleepily. As she was not being held, Clara knew the girl meant she wished to return downstairs.

"Have your tea with Suzie." Clara led Alice to a child-sized chair beside the equally miniature table.

"She'll be 'sleep afore she finishes," Suzie observed with a laugh.

"I hope so." Clara managed a smile of her own. "She is quite determined to take tea with the adults today."

"'Cause of your gentleman caller." Suzie nodded her understanding.

"Suzie," Clara lightly scolded. "He is not a gentleman caller."

Suzie looked doubtful.

"He is a gentleman, and he is a caller," Clara admitted. "But he is not a *gentleman caller*. Not in the way you are implying."

"I just thought, maybe—"

"You know me better than that." Clara, perhaps, spoke a little more forcefully than necessary. The topic of suitors and gentlemen callers and men in general was not one she wished to discuss.

Suzie had come with them from Mr. Bentford's. A chambermaid then, Suzie had agreed to serve as the girl-of-all-work at Ivy Cottage. Not precisely a promotion but certainly a more appreciated position. She and Clara had developed some semblance of a friendship, as much as could be cultivated between a servant and her mistress. The arrangement was not unpleasant for either of them.

"I only hoped, Mrs. Bentford," Suzie answered. "You deserve a good man in your life."

If Edmund hadn't been in the room and hadn't had the uncanny ability to overhear remarks not meant for his ears, Clara might have corrected any notions Suzie had about the existence of a good man. Men had been making her miserable all her life. But she still held out hope for Edmund. He was a kind and loving boy. With any luck, reaching manhood wouldn't ruin him.

"Enjoy your tea, dears." Clara kissed Edmund and Alice on the tops of their heads.

Edmund blushed at the gesture but smiled. Alice's attention was already on the plate of cake in front of her.

All was in readiness in the sitting room below. Mrs. Henderson, who came to Ivy Cottage twice a week to do the baking, would bring the tea tray in as soon as the guests arrived and then be on her way. A few cakes, a short conversation, and the visit would be over.

What on earth had possessed her to extend the invitation? she thought once more. She could just as easily have traded prayer books with the man at church the following Sunday.

She'd noticed him behind her during services each week. Alice insisted on playing peekaboo with him. Mr. Bentford would have ignored the little girl and scolded Clara for not keeping her perfectly still. The gentleman behind them had done neither. Clara hadn't been able to decide if she found the man's encouragement of Alice's antics welcoming or frustrating.

Why did he sit behind them every Sunday? What was his interest in her? In her children? Thus far, she'd managed to avoid most of the neighborhood. She much preferred blending in and going unnoticed. More than preferred it, in fact. She depended on it.

She'd enjoyed her first taste of peace and safety the past six months. The only hope she had for maintaining her hard-won freedom was keeping her life free of men and the trouble they inevitably caused.

A knock echoed off the front door. Her heart all but stopped, as it always did when someone arrived at the house. She took a deep breath, willing her heart to return to its normal rhythm.

One disadvantage of having only two servants, one who was obliged to look after the children when visitors called and the other whose duties were exclusively in the kitchen, was having to answer her own door. She never knew who was on the other side or what his intentions might be.

She made her way slowly toward the front window. Keeping out of sight, she inched back the curtain, peering out. With an immediate surge of relief, she identified Mr. and Mrs. Whittle, the vicar and his wife. She knew logically that they would be the ones standing there. But a woman in her situation could never be too careful.

"Good afternoon," she said welcomingly as the couple stepped inside.

They returned the greeting and were soon comfortably situated in the sitting room.

Mrs. Henderson brought in the tea tray and set it on the table near Clara. Just as Mrs. Henderson stepped from the room, another knock sounded.

"I will answer that before I go, ma'am," Mrs. Henderson said, sticking her head back inside the sitting room.

"Thank you." Clara's heart hammered once more. She exchanged a knowing look with Mrs. Henderson. *Check first.* Mrs. Henderson nodded her understanding. The kindhearted lady didn't know exactly why Clara was so careful of any new arrivals, but she obliged her in taking a moment to identify visitors.

In the next moment, the gentleman she'd invited stood in the doorway. He was intimidating and unfamiliar, but she wasn't truly afraid of him. Not yet. Clara was tall for a woman, but he was taller. It never ceased to amaze her that his hair was precisely the color of a polished guinea. Clara's hair was quite plainly brown. This man's was pure gold.

Shaking off the thought, Clara rose, as did the Whittles.

"Would you be so good, Mr. Whittle," Clara addressed the vicar, "as to perform an introduction? I fear this gentleman and I have not had the opportunity to be appropriately introduced."

"Of course. Of course." Mr. Whittle spoke with his usual broad smile. "Mrs. Bentford, may I present Mr. Jonquil of Havenworth."

Havenworth? The impressive estate just west of Ivy Cottage? Edmund insisted on stopping whenever they walked past to watch the many horses there. Havenworth, she had heard, was a horse-breeding farm and a highly successful one at that.

Clara curtsied as was expected, though she didn't cross any closer to him. Men were best dealt with from a distance. Even Mr. Whittle, who had proven himself harmless time and again, would have set her on edge if he didn't always come with his wife.

Mr. Jonquil executed a very proper bow. He looked displeased, his eyes surveying the room. Under his arm, he held a prayer book—Clara's, no doubt. He appeared to be muttering to himself.

Might as well attend to the business at hand, Clara told herself. "I have your prayer book just over here, Mr. Jonquil." She crossed to an end table near the fireplace, picked up the book, and turned, bracing herself to find him uncomfortably close. Mr. Jonquil, however, had not wandered an inch from the doorway.

A strange gentleman, to be sure. Clara returned to where he stood and held the book out to him. "Thank you again for inventing a means of escape for us."

Mr. Jonquil nodded and traded books with her.

"Escape?" Mr. Whittle asked, standing nearby.

"The congregation descended upon us as we left the chapel on Sunday," Clara explained, turning toward the vicar.

"Oh dear," Mrs. Whittle replied. "They do have a tendency to do that. Overly curious if you ask me."

"I would not mind for myself," Clara lied—was it particularly wrong to lie in front of a vicar? "But it does unsettle Edmund." That, at least, was the truth.

"And Mr. Jonquil provided you with an escape route?" Mr. Whittle asked.

"Yes." Clara looked once more at Mr. Jonquil. He still appeared entirely unhappy to be at Ivy Cottage. That tendency in her to prickle up, the very character trait her father had often warned her against, came to the surface once more. With a hint of cheek, she added, "Though I am afraid he did so by means of a most desperate lie. Having uttered such a glaring falsehood on the hallowed ground of the churchyard, I am quite certain Mr. Jonquil has compromised his salvation and has condemned himself to an eternity of torment and suffering. There is, I fear, no hope for him."

Clara glanced at Mr. Jonquil out of the corner of her eye, wondering what his reaction might be. His eyes continued wandering about the room, but he was smiling. It was a handsome smile and might have been far more pleasant if he didn't still appear so disapproving.

"Was it worth it, sir?" Clara asked. "Trading your eternal reward for our momentary comfort?"

"My father always said—insisted—that a good deed can make up for—No. Atone for . . ." The sentence dangled unfinished as Mr. Jonquil's mouth set in a stern line.

"'Absolve sin,'" Mr. Whittle finished for Mr. Jonquil. "The words of Peter, I believe."

"And Mr. Jonquil's father, apparently," Clara replied. "Is your father a man of the cloth as well?"

"Mr. Jonquil's father was the Earl of Lampton," Mr. Whittle answered for Mr. Jonquil, a look of near amazement on the vicar's face. "Mr. Jonquil's oldest brother now holds the title."

He hails from the aristocracy? It was little wonder, then, the man was so decidedly unimpressed with Clara's very humble dwelling.

"Forgive me for speaking so lightly of your father," Clara said, regretting her moment of cheek. "Especially in light of your loss."

Mr. Jonquil only nodded, his mouth drawn more tightly, a sure sign of discomfort and disapproval.

A moment of awkward silence passed while Clara chided herself. "Won't you please come in, Mr. Jonquil," Clara invited. A man's temper could be cooled by a satisfied stomach. "You must take your tea before it becomes cold."

He quite obviously hesitated.

"Do come sit with us, Mr. Jonquil," Mrs. Whittle added her weight to the invitation.

After another moment of apparent mental debate, Mr. Jonquil moved farther inside the room. He could have at least affected a look of approval. Perhaps he wished to make his displeasure clear.

Clara sat beside the tea tray and began pouring out for her guests. Mr. Jonquil chose a seat a little removed from the others, at Clara's small writing desk.

Not very sociable, Clara thought to herself. The observation proved prophetic. Despite the efforts of the Whittles and herself, Mr. Jonquil said very little and occupied himself, after rather quickly consuming a cup of tea, with sharpening the quills lying on the writing desk. He appeared to constantly mutter silently to himself.

Clara no longer worried about Mr. Jonquil's intentions. He obviously felt her far enough beneath his touch as to be completely unworthy of notice. It was both a stinging setdown and a tremendous relief. She far preferred a gentleman who disregarded her to a gentleman who was in relentless pursuit.

Chapter Three

Corbin rode back to Havenworth, his mind whirling. Mrs. Bentford had been a pleasant surprise. Her manners were impeccable; that much he had anticipated. He hadn't expected her obvious wit and intelligence. Mr. Whittle had casually mentioned the renewed war on the Continent, and Mrs. Bentford, unlike many in England, had a grasp of the intricacies of the situation with Napoleon and the implications of continued conflict after two decades of war.

He'd discovered she had a sense of humor. And after speaking lightly of Corbin's late father, Mrs. Bentford had immediately offered her apologies and sympathies, which seemed to indicate she was also compassionate.

It was, of course, a great deal to assume after a single call lasting less than thirty minutes, one in which he hadn't said more than a handful of words. He'd wanted to. He'd rehearsed a few things, both before arriving and as he'd sat in her sitting room. What little he'd managed had come out too uncertainly, too quietly.

From the moment he'd stepped into Mrs. Bentford's sitting room and seen her amazing eyes turn toward him, Corbin had been unable to do much beyond stand—or sit, as it were—and try to avoid making a further idiot of himself. He'd seldom been so uncomfortable, so lacking in self-assurance. Every intelligent observation he'd mentally scripted had fled from his mind.

There had to be a means of improving the impression he'd made, something he might say or do the next time they were in company with each other that would show he was not a bumbling idiot or a simpleton.

Ivy Cottage sat only a mile from Havenworth, tucked behind a copse of trees. Corbin hardly had time to reflect on his visit before arriving home, and the sight that met him at Havenworth's portico immediately shifted his thoughts.

Corbin recognized the Jonquil family arms emblazoned on the door of the traveling carriage sitting in front of his house. The earl's coronet included in the arms identified the carriage's owner as his eldest brother, Philip, the Earl of Lampton.

Corbin dismounted, allowing Johnny from the stables to lead Elf away. He took the stairs quickly, feeling his smile grow. He nodded to Simmons, the butler, as the man opened the door to allow Corbin inside.

"They are in the sitting room, Mr. Jonquil," Simmons informed him.

He headed directly there, looking forward to seeing his brother again.

"I believe I shall find myself a tartan waistcoat, my dear," Philip was saying when Corbin reached the sitting room door. "No point standing out among the local population."

"Then you had best hope the local population are horribly bruised, Philip," his wife, Sorrel, replied. "Because if you begin sporting an even more ridiculous wardrobe than you already wear, I will beat you with my walking stick."

Not what one would expect to hear from a newlywed couple, and yet Corbin was not the least surprised. And as he fully expected, both his brother and new sister-in-law were smiling at each other, sitting beside each other on a settee, completely oblivious to Corbin's presence in the doorway.

"Perhaps not the tartan, then," Philip conceded.

"We may expunge the dandy out of you yet," Sorrel said.

"That is quite an undertaking, Sorrel." He leaned closer to her, one eyebrow raised.

"Philip." She half laughed, half scolded as he leaned ever closer.

"Yes, my dear?" Philip kissed her quickly.

"Suppose Corbin were to walk in suddenly?" Sorrel pushed him back a little with her hand.

"He would be pleased to see you haven't murdered me yet." Philip leaned back at her continued insistence.

"*Surprised*, perhaps," Sorrel answered.

Corbin stepped back out of the sitting room. It would have been terribly awkward to have entered while the couple was talking about him. He waited a moment before reentering.

"There you are, Corbin," Philip said.

Corbin nodded, his usual greeting. He offered Sorrel a bow.

"We've come to brighten your day, brother." Philip smiled. Sorrel seemed to roll her eyes. "Bring a little color."

Philip gave the immediate impression of a dandy, a man with little but fashion and nonsense on his mind. Corbin knew better, as did all of the Jonquil brothers, save one. Jason, Corbin's twin, found Philip and his posturing annoying and made a point of making his feelings obvious. Corbin did not know why Philip had adopted the mannerisms he had. But since falling in love with the lady who was now his wife, Philip had begun showing signs of returning to the intelligent, thoughtful gentleman who had resided just below the surface for years.

"Simmons said you were away from Havenworth," Sorrel said.

"I was visiting. A neighbor." Corbin explained his absence.

Philip seemed surprised. Corbin did tend to keep to himself, not being very skilled as a conversationalist and always feeling a little out of his element in company. His one attempt at a Season in Town had been painfully awkward for everyone involved. Philip had never suggested Corbin try again.

"If you gentlemen will excuse me"—Sorrel awkwardly rose to her feet, hand clutching an ebony wood walking stick—"I would appreciate lying down for a time."

"Of course." Philip walked with his wife to the door of the sitting room and kissed her on the cheek before she disappeared through the doorway.

"She seems to be in pain—in more pain than before," Corbin said.

"Traveling makes her stiff." Philip still watched through the open door as his wife made her way up the stairs to the guest chambers above. There was less and less of the mindless fop in his tone. Corbin liked seeing again the brother he'd known growing up. "We've come from London, you know."

Corbin would have expected Philip to stop at the family seat, a mere fifteen miles from Havenworth.

"We received word from Dr. MacAslon, a surgeon in Edinburgh," Philip said, crossing back to the settee he had occupied before. "He and a colleague have been discussing Sorrel's leg, and he thinks he can help her. We are going directly to Scotland."

That was decidedly good news. From what Corbin understood of the new Countess of Lampton's history, she'd been severely injured by a rampaging horse a few years earlier and was plagued by continued pain, difficulty walking, and recurrent infections. It would relieve Philip's mind to have his wife's pain alleviated in any way possible.

"I hope you don't mind putting us up for the night," Philip continued. Sorrel truly had proven a sobering influence for her husband. Corbin approved of the change. "Sorrel needs to rest."

Corbin answered with a nod, though he wondered again why they hadn't stopped at their own home.

Philip briefly smiled his gratitude, but his expression remained far too grim. Corbin took a seat nearby and watched him closely. Philip almost never allowed his worry to show. Even after their father died, Philip, at only eighteen and left with the weight of a large family and estate on his shoulders, had come across as unfailingly confident and assured.

He seemed to notice Corbin's scrutiny and chuckled a little. "I've turned into a doting husband, haven't I? It will be the next trend, you realize. Husbands throughout the *ton* will waste away, worrying over their wives."

Marriages in the *ton* were too often based on mutual apathy and seldom included doting in any form. If anyone could set a trend, however, it would be Philip. The Earl of Lampton, though generally lauded as not entirely intelligent, did have a sense of fashion just eccentric enough to be famous.

Philip's smile and humor faded. "It will be a difficult surgery." His brows furrowed in concern. "And terribly painful. Her leg will have to be broken again and reset. Though she is going to great lengths to hide it, Sorrel is nervous. And there is no guarantee the operation will be successful."

"Can I do anything?" Corbin offered, realizing he likely could do nothing but wishing otherwise.

"Actually, yes." Philip straightened and resumed the air of an earl and a man in control of every situation. "I do not plan to bring Sorrel back until I am certain she has fully recovered. We could be in Scotland for a month or more. Layton and Marion will be in Derbyshire for at least another week. And Stanley just left for Tallow to rejoin his regiment, thanks to Napoleon's escape from Elba." Philip rose and began pacing. "Jason, no doubt, won't budge from Town, regardless of the motivation." Philip shook his head.

Why is it that Philip and Jason don't get along? Corbin wondered for not the first time.

"Harry, despite being a new cleric, is still relatively young," Philip said. "And Charlie is only seventeen."

Seventeen—only a year younger than Philip had been when Father died.

"I am leaving behind a family in need of looking after," Philip said. "Sorrel, despite her insistence otherwise, will need my attention during her recovery. Layton ought to be permitted time with his new bride. So I need you to take charge of things while I'm away. Check on Mater now and then.

Make sure Charlie isn't giving her too much grief. She'll have Caroline with her at the Park while Layton is gone, so she'll be run ragged as it is."

Corbin nodded his consent. Havenworth was an easy distance from Lampton Park. He knew he could be spared now and then.

"I will feel more at ease knowing you are nearby to help with the family in my absence."

"I would do whatever—would do anything for—" The words weren't coming out right.

Philip seemed to understand the avowal Corbin couldn't manage to get out intact. "I too would do anything in the world for this family." Philip gave him a look that told him, beyond any doubt, that he had sacrificed more for his brothers and Mater than any of them realized.

Corbin couldn't remember Philip ever turning to him for assistance with anything. Layton or Jason, even, had more often been the brothers looked to in difficulty. Corbin liked the idea that Philip trusted him—Philip, who had pulled the Jonquil family through the death of their father, had held them together through countless difficulties in the years since.

"I'll look in on Mater," Corbin promised.

"Thank you." Philip immediately looked relieved. Then he smiled the way he always did when he was up to some mischief. "How are things in the neighborhood, Corbin?"

Why did Philip seem to find that question so amusing? Corbin shrugged a reply.

"You were visiting a neighbor, you said," Philip went on. "Anyone in particular?"

Corbin couldn't hold back a smile. Philip could be remarkably pointed. "Mrs. Bentford," Corbin answered quietly.

"And *Mr.* Bentford?" Philip asked, studying his fingernails.

Corbin didn't answer but looked away.

"It is she, isn't it?" A hint of excitement entered Philip's voice. "She is the lady you mentioned to Layton."

"He told you?" Corbin shifted uncomfortably.

"Corbin." Philip chuckled. "You have never once in your twenty-five years shown the slightest interest in a female, except when you were six and were in love with Bridget Sarvol for a few months, until you found out she didn't like horses. Of course Layton told me."

He heard no pity or laughter in Philip's voice.

"So have you finally been introduced to Mrs. . . . *Bentford*, was it?"

Corbin nodded.

"And?" Philip pressed.

It didn't go well. But Corbin didn't express the thought out loud.

"What did you talk about?"

Corbin cringed inwardly. *Talk about?* Corbin had never held an actual conversation with a virtual stranger. His business dealings were conducted as much as possible in writing.

"Oh, lud." Philip chuckled, apparently realizing his error. "You must have done something. I can't imagine the two of you simply sitting in silence for the space of an afternoon call."

"Tea," Corbin answered. "With the vicar. And his wife."

"And during tea you . . . ?" Philip attempted to lead the conversation.

"Cut her quills," Corbin answered under his breath.

"Cut quills?" Philip answered with obvious disbelief.

"They needed cutting." They'd been terribly dull. He'd wanted to do something helpful.

"So now she is probably convinced you were bored out of your mind." Philip shook his head.

"Truly?" Corbin felt uneasy all over again.

"Truly," Philip insisted.

Corbin rose to his feet, making his way tensely to the windows of the sitting room. Did Mrs. Bentford think he'd been bored? Or unhappy? Nervous, yes. But there was a vast deal of enjoyment to be had just watching Mrs. Bentford as she went about her duties as hostess. Her grace and smile had been entrancing. Listening to her conversation had been captivating.

No, he hadn't been bored or unhappy in the least.

"Or she may simply forget you were at her home in the first place." Philip did not particularly ease Corbin's mind.

He certainly didn't want Mrs. Bentford to be as oblivious to his existence as she had heretofore been. "What do I do now?" Corbin asked no one in particular.

"Make your presence known," Philip suggested, joining him at the window.

Corbin looked at him. *What does he mean by that?*

"Sorrel and I did not get along when we first met," Philip said. Corbin smiled—that was certainly true. "But I guarantee she didn't overlook me. Catching a lady's eye is half the battle, brother."

"Just . . . just getting her attention?" It seemed too simple.

"Once she's noticed you, she's more likely to fall head-over-heels for you. That will never happen if you blend into the wall."

"How?" Corbin had never captured anyone's attention before.

Philip grinned.

Corbin got the sudden impression he would not like whatever was tossing around in Philip's head.

Chapter Four

THE CONGREGATION GREW UNUSUALLY TALKATIVE just before Mr. Whittle began his sermon. Something had set the citizens of Grompton chattering, but Clara couldn't say what.

"They sound like bees," Edmund whispered to her not long after the conversations around them began.

Clara smiled back at him. "They certainly do."

As the vicar's sermon continued, a feeling of barely suppressed energy filled the air as if the worshipers were anxious to get on with their discussions.

Alice had, once again, taken it upon herself to entertain Mr. Jonquil. Clara had noticed him behind them—his head of molten gold was difficult to miss. She'd hardly needed to turn her head. The briefest of glances in his direction had identified him.

He had acted so strangely at tea a few days earlier. It seemed as if he couldn't quit Ivy Cottage and her company fast enough. While Clara didn't want to be warding off a suitor, she didn't appreciate being looked down on either.

The moment Mr. Whittle closed his remarks and the services ended, the conversations erupted again. What was everyone talking about?

Clara guided the children from the chapel, hoping that whatever occupied the neighborhood would continue to do so until they could make good their escape. There would be no prayer-book ruse to rescue her this week, and she truly did not wish to be accosted. Her life and her past were for her alone and were not open to the evaluation of the curious.

Only a few steps from the door of the chapel, Alice pulled free of Clara's grip and ran around the edge of the pressing crowd. So unexpected was Alice's defection that Clara lost a few precious moments in stunned surprise before she and Edmund followed Alice's path. The girl had managed to weave a bit into the crowd, making following her a little tricky.

"Mrs. Bentford," a cringe-inducing voice greeted her.

She did not stop to converse.

Mr. Finley was often in Grompton. She had seen him importune more than one woman, preferring, as near as she could tell, those whose situations or personalities made them most vulnerable. Despite her best efforts, he had somehow sensed that in her. He followed her about if they were ever in Grompton at the same time, and he tracked her down after church when he attended. She only hoped his attentions would never go beyond bothersome.

Clara continued navigating the crowd, attempting to follow the path Alice had taken, unwilling to call out to the child and draw extra attention from those who were far too busy gossiping to take much notice of her. All she wanted, all she'd ever wanted, was to be left alone.

"Mrs. Bentford." Mr. Finley caught up with her once more, stepping in her line of progress and effectively stopping her in her tracks.

She forced herself to remain calm. He was too forward, too sure of himself, and too often threw himself in her way. But thus far he'd not gone beyond that. He had never raised a hand to her, hadn't taken to verbal threats. In that respect, he was better than any of the other men who had ever been part of her life.

"You are blocking my path," Clara told him calmly.

Edmund took refuge behind her, clutching her hand the way he did when he was worried or afraid. How Clara wished the boy had a role model, someone to teach him how to be a man, but a good one.

Mr. Finley doffed his tall beaver hat and smiled quite handsomely. Behind the benign expression, though, was the very clear belief that she should be falling at his feet, flattered at his attentions. He was too arrogant by half. "I only wished to give you good day," he said.

"Good day." Clara returned the greeting as a farewell and moved quickly around him, Edmund clinging to her like a bat to the eaves.

"I do not like him," Edmund whispered to her.

"Neither do I." Why couldn't the world just leave her be?

"There is Alice." Edmund pointed ahead of them.

Clara followed his gesture and, sure enough, saw Alice, hands clasped to her mouth, laughing. Her tiny giggles gave way to fits of uncontrolled laughter.

"Alice," Clara called out to her.

Alice spun at the sound and, still laughing, toddled back to her. Clara knelt on the ground before her. "You know you are not to run off, dearest."

"So funny." Alice sputtered through her fingers.

"Dearest." Clara attempted to chide the wayward girl, but Alice's laughter had infected Edmund. In the next moment, Clara laughed herself, though she was at a loss to explain why. "Just what, Alice, is so funny?"

"Mister," she answered through another sputter.

"Mister?"

"Funny."

"And who is Mr. Funny?" Clara asked, her own laughter impossible to hold back now. Alice had a laugh that instantly sent others into fits of hysteria.

"Mr. Jonquil, I believe." Mr. Finley's voice answered the question.

Why couldn't the infuriating man simply take his leave?

"Yes," Mr. Finley continued. "Mr. Jonquil can, at this moment, only be described as excessively funny."

Clara looked up at that, not at Mr. Finley but in the direction from which Alice had only just come. Mr. Jonquil stood there but not at all as she remembered him. When he had come for tea, he had been quite appropriately inconspicuous in his appearance, his clothing the subdued colors considered quite suitable for a gentleman. Indeed, his dress had always been unexceptional.

But there, in the churchyard, stood Mr. Jonquil, clad in a severely cut coat in a surprising shade of bright blue, paired with a waistcoat of orange-and-blue stripes. His watch chain must have held a half dozen fobs. His shirt points all but eliminated the line of his jaw.

"Mr. Funny." Alice giggled. Edmund laughed as well.

Clara only barely managed to bite down an answering laugh but could not keep a smile from reaching her face. He really did look utterly absurd, and Alice's infectious laugh was not helping.

Mr. Jonquil's look became instantly tenser, his brows knit, mouth turned down in a frown. Clara wanted to laugh simply at the sourness of his expression but found she could not.

"It appears, Jonquil, you have been taking lessons from your brother." Mr. Finley chuckled the way children did when taunting their playmates. "You look every bit as ridiculous as Lampton does on a daily basis."

The tenseness around Mr. Jonquil's mouth increased with each word Mr. Finley spoke. Clara felt unexpectedly compelled to speak up, regardless of how ridiculous Mr. Jonquil actually looked. She despised bullies.

"On the contrary, Mr. Finley," she said. "I do believe Mr. Jonquil looks very well in blue. A man with brown eyes, for example, would look quite unhandsome in such a vivid color."

As Mr. Finley's eyes were decidedly brown, he seemed to bristle at this remark. Clara kept her expression as innocent as possible until the frustrating man took himself off. She felt a moment of triumph at that.

She turned to offer her apologies to Mr. Jonquil for Alice's unfortunate fit of hilarity, but when she glanced back in his direction, she saw him in the lane just beyond the churchyard, mounting his horse.

He had offered not so much as a "by your leave" or a "farewell." Certainly an unsociable gentleman. Perhaps he simply disdained to socialize with his neighbors. The son of an earl was, no doubt, accustomed to much higher company than that found in Grompton. He might not have appreciated her defense of him, but Clara fully meant to be proud of herself. There was once a time she would have cowered in silence.

"Come along, children," she said. "I believe Suzie will be making sweet biscuits this afternoon. We don't want to arrive too late to help her clean the spoon."

That set the children to nearly running. Clara's longer legs made keeping up with them a simple task. She found she had a great deal of time to think over the morning as they wound their way down the lanes leading west from Grompton.

She no longer wondered at the whispers that had echoed off the chapel walls and around the churchyard. Mr. Jonquil generally blended into his surroundings. She herself probably would not have noticed him if he didn't sit behind them week after week. If she was being completely honest, his golden halo of hair drew her attention more often than it ought. That morning, however, his attire had drawn the attention of all the town.

What had brought about so odd a choice of clothing? It didn't suit him, despite what she'd told Mr. Finley. Clara felt a hot flush spread quickly across her face. *That* wasn't entirely true. The color perfectly suited him. His eyes were certainly blue—another thing about him she couldn't help noticing—but the blue of his coat had rendered them breathtaking.

"Can we stop, please?" Edmund asked, pulling on her hand.

Clara jumped from her thoughts and looked around, momentarily disoriented. They were not far from the turnoff to Ivy Cottage and were standing at the edge of Havenworth property. Clara followed Edmund's eager eyes toward the enclosed field. Several gorgeous horses capered about, manes furrowing as they bounded and jumped. Clara appreciated the pleasant picture they made. Edmund, however, stood positively mesmerized.

"I wish I had a horse," Edmund whispered, leaning against the fence. "I would be a good rider, I know it."

Her heart squeezed at the longing in his voice. When did Edmund ever ask for anything? He willingly went about his studies. He watched out for Alice. The poor boy had endured Mr. Bentford.

All he ever wished for was a horse.

Clara could not begin to afford one. She forced down the lump that formed in her throat. "Someday, Edmund," she promised him, squeezing his overly slender shoulders. "Someday you will have your horse."

They watched the graceful animals for Clara knew not how long. By the time she pulled Edmund away from the sight, Alice had fallen asleep in her arms. Edmund continued their journey but reluctantly so, despite the promise of biscuits.

There had to be a way, Clara told herself. There had to be a way to give Edmund the only thing he'd ever wanted.

* * *

If they only ate three times a week, it might be possible. Clara laid her quill on the writing desk beside the sheet of parchment that contained her calculations. Two days had passed since Edmund had stood wistfully at the Havenworth fence.

She'd gone into Grompton that afternoon after the children had finished their lessons and had inquired after the price of various aspects of keeping a horse: shoeing, a saddle, bridle, feed. Without even taking into account the purchase price of such an animal, nor the cost of stabling—either constructing a stable at Ivy Cottage or paying to have the animal stabled elsewhere—she hadn't the means to keep so much as a pony, let alone a horse Edmund could grow in to.

She exhaled a quick puff of breath and rose from the desk, crossing the sitting room to the tall eastern windows. The sun had long since set, and the children were sleeping in their rooms above. Even Suzie had retired for the night, leaving Clara the sole member of the household still awake. She looked through the windows into the darkness outside.

Dear, sweet Edmund.

"There has to be a way to secure a mount for the boy," Clara told herself yet again.

Far into the dark night a light shimmered, no doubt flickering through the many windows of Havenworth, too distant for details but near enough for the light to be seen. That estate must have seemed the very picture of heaven to young Edmund. It was a beautiful home, small when compared to the grand estates of the aristocracy but far too grand to be labeled "quaint" as Ivy Cottage was. The grounds were lush, the trees near the house tall and majestic. Havenworth's stables were at least as expansive as the house itself—home to quite a number of fine horses and ponies.

One of the distant lights extinguished. Havenworth was turning in for the night. Did Mr. Jonquil realize she could see his home from Ivy Cottage? She imagined not. He certainly had more important things to do with his time. He'd made that abundantly clear during his afternoon call the week before.

Clara leaned against the window frame. If she thought on the problem long enough, surely a solution would present itself.

Edmund had inherited an income from his late father. Most of that would not come to him until he reached his majority, some fourteen years down the road. In the meantime, the boy received a quarterly stipend, enough that, were she to tap deeply into the account, they could live more comfortably than they were. Clara, however, was determined not to use a single halfpenny more than she absolutely had to. That money was all he had to secure his future and allow him to attend Eton without the degradation of doing so as a charity student. Despite their straitened circumstances, Edmund had something to fall back on. Alice didn't even have that.

She would one day require a dowry if she ever meant to marry. A dowry did not guarantee marital happiness, Clara knew well, but she would not force Alice into a life of misery for the sake of connections or family pride. She valued her children's happiness above such things. So if Alice never met anyone she could trust enough to treat her with kindness and respect, she would need an income to live on. Here was yet another expense Clara was ill-prepared to meet.

The dowry could wait. But Edmund really ought to learn to ride. She simply could not think of a way to accomplish the feat.

The last light at Havenworth extinguished, bathing the countryside in black. Only the single candle lit in the sitting room broke the darkness. She took the candle and slowly made her way up the stairs to her room. She undressed methodically, her mind heavy, and sat on the edge of her bed in her warm, flannel nightdress, her bare toes cold in the chilly night air.

She blew out the candle and lay back on her pillow. She had her faults, heaven knew, but she had always been determined. Somehow, she would give her children what they deserved.

She just simply had no idea how.

Chapter Five

PHILIP AND SORREL HAD REACHED Scotland and would be meeting with Dr. MacAslon in a few days' time. Not an ounce of the frustration Corbin felt with his eldest brother abated as he read the letter that had only just arrived. Five days had passed since the episode at church.

"You need to catch her eye," Philip had said. "Stand out from the crowd," he'd insisted.

Corbin, like a dolt, had gone along with the entire harebrained idea. He and Philip were of a size, similar enough in build for Corbin to borrow a few items of clothing. Years spent at the stables, working as hard as any of his stable hands, had given Corbin a little more mass than his brother, rendering the attire more form-fitting than it was on Philip. But, Philip assured him, a tight fit was considered quite stylish in Town.

Philip had been right on one count. Mrs. Bentford had certainly noticed him. If the fits of laughter she and her children had burst into upon first sight of him were any indication, he had certainly stood out. And he hadn't failed to notice the rest of the congregation taking note of the ridiculous picture he'd made. Corbin couldn't remember the last time Mr. Whittle had been required to stand at the pulpit for so long waiting for the chapel to quiet down.

When Philip came back from Scotland, Corbin was going to kill him.

He dropped the letter onto his desk and leaned back in his chair, spinning his sealing stamp in his hand. He'd made a complete and utter fool of himself, that much was certain. Half the stable staff had ribbed him over his mishap. He hadn't yet returned to Grompton. He wasn't sure he'd ever venture back.

Eventually, he realized, he'd have to face *her* again. Mrs. Bentford was his neighbor. He could see Ivy Cottage from the windows of Havenworth.

Corbin got to his feet and moved to the windows, passing his sealing stamp from one hand to the other as he thought. He'd simply wanted to capture her attention but not at all in the way he had. Perhaps he ought to think of a means of redeeming himself, making a better impression. Nothing came to mind.

The door to the library opened. Corbin turned to see Simmons step inside.

"Mrs. Bentford is here to see you, Mr. Jonquil," the butler informed him.

Corbin dropped the stamp.

"On a matter of business," Simmons clarified.

"Mrs. Bentford?" he asked in shocked astonishment.

Simmons nodded.

"Here?"

"Yes, sir."

Corbin picked the stamp off the floor, then crossed back to his desk. He set the stamp down, but it rolled off the edge. A second try saw it settled securely on the desk. Corbin took a deliberate breath.

"Where—Where have you put her?"

"I suggested the sitting room, sir. But as she has come to discuss a matter of business, Mrs. Bentford insisted she meet with you in whichever room you conduct your business."

"In here?" Had his voice actually just cracked?

"She is only a few paces outside the door, Mr. Jonquil."

Absolutely no response came to mind. Corbin could do little more than stare at the man. Mrs. Bentford? At Havenworth? Just outside the door to his library?

Corbin looked around. At least the room was clean. Except for the desk. Corbin quickly straightened the papers there.

"Shall I show her in, Mr. Jonquil?" Simmons asked in a voice that hinted that he ought to have done so already.

Corbin nodded.

Simmons stepped out the door. Corbin smoothed the creases in his jacket and waistcoat, thankful he was wearing his own clothing and not the dandified fashions Philip had so long favored. *How do you do*? he silently practiced. *Good day, Mrs. Bentford.* He tried a different approach. *So good to see you again.*

"Mrs. Bentford, sir," Simmons announced from the door.

Corbin stepped from his desk, forcing a swallow and a breath. *Good day, Mrs. Bentford. How do you do?*

She stepped inside.

Corbin took a breath and looked over at her. The breath caught in his throat. How was it possible for a woman to become more beautiful with each encounter? He ought to be growing more immune to her presence, feeling the impact less forcefully. Instead, he found himself dissolving into a helpless heap faster with each meeting.

Good day, Mrs. Bentford. Good day, Mrs. Bentford. "Good—um—good day."

"And to you, Mr. Jonquil."

After a bow and a curtsy, they stood in complete silence. Corbin did his utmost to not look at her without appearing to be not looking at her. He knew that the moment his eyes met her startlingly green ones, he would freeze, unable to look away or form a coherent sentence. *How do you do?* Except she would probably return the inquiry, and he'd have to answer her. *I am well, thank you.*

"Forgive me, Mr. Jonquil." Mrs. Bentford broke the awkward silence between them. "I know it is not customary for a lady, alone, to call on a gentleman, but I assure you I have come to discuss a matter of business."

"Business?"

"In regard to my Edmund," she added.

"Edmund?" He had begun to sound like a poorly trained parrot.

"Edmund is a quiet boy, given to sedate pursuits. He spends his days indoors, engrossed in books and such."

Corbin had never before seen her appear uncertain. The sight tugged at his heart in much the same way her smile had so many weeks before. There was undeniable bravery in her posture and in her willingness to meet with a relatively unfamiliar gentleman over a matter of business.

"While I approve of his efforts to improve his mind," she continued, "I cannot help feeling he is in desperate need of exercise and activity as well."

Corbin had no idea what she was getting at but found himself entranced just the same. She had a very calm, soothing tone even in her obvious discomfort.

"Edmund has, for years now, shown an interest in horses."

"Horses?" Could he manage nothing beyond mindlessly repeating what she said? *I like horses too.* That sounded childish. *Does he have a horse?* No, he didn't recall seeing a stable at Ivy Cottage. *Does he ride?* "Does he ride?"

"No." Something of an embarrassed flush spread through her cheeks at the quiet admission. "Mr. Bentford did not keep any animals suitable for a child. I haven't any horses myself now."

"You wish to purchase a pony? For Edmund?" Was that the business she'd referred to?

Her color intensified, but she raised her chin and spoke with almost palpable dignity. "I haven't the means to purchase nor keep a horse or a pony." She looked him in the eye as if daring him to pity or look down on her for her relative poverty. "I hope, instead, to negotiate something of a trade."

A trade? That was unexpected. Corbin couldn't even think of a response.

The look of uncertainty Mrs. Bentford had worn during her earlier recitation passed once more through her eyes. Corbin had a very strong feeling that this transaction was costing her a great deal of pride. Few people enjoyed admitting to their limited finances or inability to make a purchase others took quite for granted. "Please sit, Mrs. Bentford," Corbin abruptly offered, speaking the moment the thought passed through his mind. He really ought to have made the offer earlier.

"Thank you." Mrs. Bentford took a seat on the other side of Corbin's desk.

It would be awkward sitting across the desk from her. Corbin opted, instead, for a seat nearer hers. He sat, heart pounding, thoughts spinning.

What precisely is this trade? He could probably manage to say that. "Explain this trade," he said. "Please." It was close, at least. But, then, so was she. Other than church on Sundays, he'd never sat so near her. He forced himself not to look into her eyes.

"I had hoped you might have a job or two, something a seven-year-old might reasonably be taught to perform." She looked away from him as she spoke. That made the conversation easier for him. The feel of her gaze on him was a tremendous barrier to his concentration. "Something in the stables, with the horses. Brushing them or mucking—"

"Mucking is hard work for a seven-year-old," Corbin said, knowing how difficult that dirtiest of stable jobs was. Had that come out as a complete sentence? Corbin sat in momentary shock.

"Perhaps not mucking, then." Mrs. Bentford looked evermore uncomfortable. She glanced up at him quite unexpectedly, and Corbin was captured. "Surely a young boy could be useful in the stables."

Corbin had spent most of his boyhood in the stables. He nodded.

Mrs. Bentford's mouth slowly turned up in an answering smile.

Corbin couldn't decide which was more mesmerizing, her emerald eyes or her smiling lips. He managed to look away only by rising and moving across the room. *I could certainly find chores enough to occupy him.* Maybe, *There are plenty of chores a young child can perform.* "There are plenty—plenty of chores a young child can do," he said from the window.

"I realize you have a more than adequate staff."

Corbin disliked the apprehension he heard in her voice. He wished her to be comfortable with him despite the fact that he felt monumentally uncomfortable with her.

"I had hoped Edmund might be permitted to perform a few chores in trade, sir," Mrs. Bentford said. "I hoped he might trade his labor for a chance to ride."

"Edmund wishes to ride?"

"It is the only thing he has ever asked of me." There was a catch in her voice.

Corbin turned to look at her. He'd never before seen a slump in her shoulders. Mrs. Bentford always carried herself with an air of determination and control. But sitting there in his library, she seemed weighed down, burdened.

He wanted to say something but couldn't decide what. His father's words swam through his mind the way they always did when he anxiously debated what to say. "Words cannot be unsaid," Father had told him. Corbin had never forgotten that caution.

What could he say? *Edmund seems happy, even if he doesn't ride.* Or, *Is there anything I can do for* you, *Mrs. Bentford?* No, that would be too presumptuous.

Mrs. Bentford spoke before Corbin had a chance to decide what, if anything, he ought to say to her. "He does not know how to ride," she said. "I do not wish to take time from your stable hands. I had hoped if he did a few chores, it might allow someone time to teach him."

"I will teach him," Corbin offered on the spot. Again he'd managed a complete sentence and without a great deal of prior thought.

"Oh, I couldn't." Mrs. Bentford stood instantly, shaking her head. "Your time, sir, must be extremely valuable. You have this estate to run and oversee."

"But if . . . if he—" Corbin took a breath, telling himself firmly not to be an idiot. *If he is willing to work, I will see to it that he learns to ride.*

He repeated that a couple times. "If he is willing to come . . . come and work, then I will see to it that he learns. To ride."

"I hadn't intended to disrupt your personal schedule, Mr. Jonquil." She had begun pacing, continuing to shake her head. "Edmund is unused to physical exertion, and while I assure you he will put himself into his chores completely, I doubt he will produce results worthy of anything beyond a few words of advice from a stable hand. Certainly not enough to justify your taking time with him."

"It—I wouldn't—" *Think, Corbin. I would enjoy teaching the boy to ride.*

"I have no desire to be indebted," Mrs. Bentford insisted. She looked back at him.

Those eyes. Corbin once again found breathing and thinking difficult. He shook his head, hoping she understood he was negating her objection. No words were forming, no thoughts registering.

"If he came, could someone take time with him?" Mrs. Bentford asked.

Corbin nodded immediately, emphatically. He himself would take time with the boy.

"He does his lessons in the mornings," Mrs. Bentford said. "I do not wish to interrupt his studies."

Edmund can come after he has his lunch. All that came out was, "Afternoon?"

"And he will be retrieved before dinner."

Corbin nodded.

"And if the trade proves too disproportional, you will tell me," Mrs. Bentford insisted. "I have no desire to place a burden on you. This is your livelihood."

He nodded once more.

Then Mrs. Bentford smiled at him, and every lucid thought fled from his mind. He'd lost his heart to Mrs. Bentford over that smile.

"Thank you, Mr. Jonquil." She crossed toward the door but turned back before exiting. "Thank you so very much." Her green eyes danced and sparkled.

He couldn't even respond, skewered as he was.

"Thank you," she said once more, and then she left.

A moment or two passed before Corbin recovered enough to even turn back to face the window. He watched Mrs. Bentford walk swiftly from the front door of Havenworth and down the path that led back to the road that would take her to Ivy Cottage. He watched until the trees along the road blocked her from view.

A smile crept across his face. She hadn't even mentioned his ridiculous appearance on Sunday last. And though he hadn't exactly been articulate, he'd held up his end of the conversation to an extent. It was an accomplishment most gentlemen would not even notice.

Perhaps he had redeemed himself at least a little.

Chapter Six

"Am I doing this right?" young Edmund asked, running the stiff-bristled brush along Happy Helper's side.

"A little more force," Corbin replied.

Edmund nodded and furrowed his brows in concentration.

"Very good." Corbin watched the boy a moment longer. Edmund reminded him so much of himself as a lad—anxious to do every little thing correctly, eager to learn, and exceptionally quiet.

"He is a very small horse." Edmund continued his rhythmic brushing.

"*She*," Corbin corrected.

"Oh." No offense seemed taken, no injured pride.

"And Happy Helper is a pony, not a horse," Corbin added.

"Isn't a pony just a baby horse?" Edmund paused in his work to look up at him. He didn't have Mrs. Bentford's green eyes, but something in his countenance reminded Corbin of her.

"No," Corbin answered. "Ponies are small. But they don't grow big." He joined Edmund at Happy Helper's side, stroking the pony's neck. "And a pony's legs are shorter. They have smaller heads."

"So Happy Helper will never grow up?" Edmund asked.

"She *is* grown up," Corbin corrected.

"Like how Suzie is grown up, but she is smaller than Aunt Clara?" Edmund asked, the hand holding his brush hanging forgotten at his side.

Corbin nodded, wondering who Suzie was and if Edmund's Aunt Clara was related to Mrs. Bentford or was from his father's side of the family.

Edmund began brushing again. He had proven himself a hard worker. He was anxious over the animals Corbin had placed, even momentarily, in his care. One could tell a lot about a person by watching how they treated those in their care, be they human or animal.

Edmund's strokes slowed, his eyes wandering toward the paddock. Corbin looked as well and smiled, knowing exactly what had drawn the boy's attention.

"That's Devil's Advocate," he said. The night-black gelding was showing off quite shamelessly. He was Philip's horse through and through.

"He's beautiful," the boy said in obvious awe.

The stable hands were running Devil's Advocate—the gelding was too high-spirited to be cooped up in a stall. The animal had good carriage and was well proportioned and spirited into the bargain.

"Johnny," Corbin quietly called to one of the stable hands nearby. "Finish brushing Happy Helper?"

Johnny grinned at the awestruck boy and nodded. The entire staff had taken to Edmund almost on sight. He seemed to worship every person connected to the Havenworth stables.

Corbin led Edmund out to the fence. The boy stood beside him, watching the display. Corbin held back an amused chuckle. He must have looked precisely like that as a child watching the horses in the Lampton Park stables.

Devil's Advocate kicked halfheartedly at a groom approaching him from behind.

"That man shouldn't sneak up on him," Edmund said, his brow furrowed quite seriously.

"Why not?" Corbin knew perfectly well that Edmund was correct but wondered if the boy understood.

"The black horse only kicks at him to tell him not to be impertinent," was the authoritative reply.

The boy obviously had a sense when it came to horses, something of a natural understanding.

"Absolutely right." Corbin shook his head in amazement. "Devil's Advocate has a very fiery temperament. Don't approach him. A single kick from a horse that size could . . . could break one of your bones or worse."

"My arm was broken once." The experience had clearly been an unpleasant one for Edmund. "I don't want to have any more broken bones."

"Then we'll leave the care of the black horse to the stable hands," Corbin said.

Edmund gave him a grateful glance. "Your horse is red," he said. "Whose horse is the black one?"

"My brother's."

"Does your brother have a fiery tempera–temmerem–tempermin?" Edmund asked.

"No. But Philip—that's my brother—knows how to handle Devil's Advocate."

Corbin watched Jim, his right-hand man at the stables, calling out to Devil's Advocate. *From Diablo Negro out of Night Wanderer.* He knew the pedigree of every horse foaled at Havenworth, but Devil's Advocate he would never forget.

Philip had somehow arranged for Diablo Negro, the most sought-after stud stallion in all of Britain, to come to Havenworth in the early days of Corbin's enterprise. His first five foals had come from that miracle of a negotiation. He'd sold all five for astounding prices, but Devil's Advocate had been the prize. If not for the small slash of white across the horse's nose, it would have been pure black, and Corbin might have asked twice as much. As it was, Philip had paid more than Corbin had asked.

"I would like to raise a horse," Edmund said, sighing wistfully. "A whole herd."

"I always wanted to as well." The memory of his own longing at a tender age struck Corbin forcibly. Father had left specific instructions in his will regarding Corbin's future. Philip and Father had discussed what could be done to make Corbin's dream of a stud farm feasible. He was given the chance to buy one of the unentailed Lampton properties over time using the profits from his farm. He'd begun his efforts at Havenworth within months of finishing at Eton. That was eight years ago. Another successful year and he would own the property outright.

"Aunt Clara says I'm going to be a gentleman," Edmund said unexpectedly. "Gentlemen can raise horses, can't they?"

"They can," Corbin replied. He had worried about the same thing when he was young. Horse breeding, his father assured him, was one of the occupations acceptable for a gentleman.

"She says I have to go to school first." A hint of a pout tugged at his mouth.

"I went to school."

"Truly?" For the first time since his attention had been captured by Devil's Advocate, Edmund pulled his gaze away from the horse and looked up at Corbin. "Did you like school?"

"Yes," Corbin replied. "And no."

"Were you scared to go?" Edmund asked quietly.

"A little," Corbin answered. The boy was easy to talk to. "But my brothers were there. That helped."

"I don't have brothers." Edmund turned his gaze back to the paddock.

"But I didn't have a sister," Corbin answered. "You do."

"Not really." The boy shrugged. "She's Aunt Clara's baby. But I am like her brother. I take care of her and play with her. So that makes me almost a brother, doesn't it?"

Aunt Clara's baby? Corbin was thoroughly confused. Alice looked far too much like Mrs. Bentford to be anyone else's child.

"Where is your Aunt Clara?" Corbin's curiosity grew by leaps and bounds.

He received a completely baffled look in response. "Probably at home."

"Where is that?"

Still that look of confusion. Edmund silently pointed to the west, toward Ivy Cottage.

"Mrs. Bentford?" Corbin thought he already knew the answer. "She . . . she is your Aunt Clara?"

Edmund nodded with a look that indicated he thought Corbin ought to have known as much.

"And you live with her."

"Because my parents are dead." Edmund spoke without sadness or self-pity.

So that was the answer to the mystery that had so captured the imagination of the neighborhood. Edmund, who was by all accounts too old to be Mrs. Bentford's son, was, in fact, her nephew.

"My father is dead as well." Corbin could not say why he offered such a personal piece of information. He rarely talked about personal matters, even with his own family. The words had just come out.

"Do you miss him?" the boy asked.

Corbin nodded.

"I don't miss my father," Edmund said. "I don't remember him much. Only Aunt Clara. And Mr. Bentford." His countenance dropped at the mention of his uncle. "But Aunt Clara says I don't have to remember him if I don't want to." Edmund dug his toe into the grass and dropped his gaze.

"Do you? Want to remember him?" The boy's obvious discomfort when recalling Mrs. Bentford's late husband worried Corbin. Had the man been cruel? Or simply indifferent?

Edmund shook his head. "He wasn't very nice," he whispered.

Corbin put an arm around the boy's shoulders. They stood silently, watching Devil's Advocate prancing around, snorting and snapping at Jim.

He wasn't very nice. Corbin squeezed Edmund's shoulders. Would Mrs. Bentford—*Clara*, Corbin reminded himself—describe her late husband that way as well?

"Was your father nice?" Edmund quietly asked.

"Very nice."

"Will you tell me about him someday?"

Corbin wavered. He never spoke to anyone about his father, not even to his own brothers. His memories of that man were far too personal to share. Yet he sensed in Edmund a need to know that there were men he could admire and hope to emulate.

Before Corbin could answer, Edmund pulled away from him. "Aunt Clara!" he shouted, running along the paddock fence in the direction of the house.

Corbin's heart suddenly flew to his throat. He wasn't even wearing a coat. A gentleman never appeared in company in only his shirtsleeves. Edmund pulled his aunt Clara by the hand toward the spot where Corbin stood.

He must have looked every bit as ridiculous as he had on Sunday. So much for better impressions.

"I hope Edmund was a good worker," Clara said as she reached his side.

Afraid he would actually call her Clara, for he could no longer think of her as Mrs. Bentford, Corbin only nodded.

"Can I come tomorrow?" Edmund asked him.

Corbin shook his head. "Tomorrow is Sunday," he explained, then began walking back to the stables. *Only in my shirtsleeves. Must I always make a complete fool of myself? It's no wonder she hasn't given me a second glance.*

"Monday, then?" Clara asked.

Corbin nodded without looking back at her.

"Good-bye, Mr. Jonquil," Edmund called out to him.

Corbin glanced over his shoulder and offered a slight smile. "Good-bye, Edmund," he replied, then fled for the obscurity of the stables.

Why hadn't Clara sent the young serving girl to fetch Edmund? The girl had brought him earlier. If Corbin had realized Clara herself would be coming, he would have seen to it that he looked presentable. He would have practiced a greeting, decided on a topic of conversation.

He dropped onto a stool near the door of the stable, where he could watch Clara and Edmund walk away from the paddock. He probably should have walked with them or offered a carriage to take them back to Ivy Cottage.

He doubted any of his brothers would have bungled things so quickly, so thoroughly. Corbin rubbed his face with his hands. He was failing miserably.

Chapter Seven

Obviously Mr. Jonquil didn't feel she was worth his time or notice. He didn't say a single word to her. Clara couldn't, for the life of her, understand why he so wholly disapproved of her. They were not well acquainted. He'd noticeably stiffened when he'd seen her arrive. He'd left with only the briefest backward glance and parting word for Edmund.

Edmund, on the other hand, hadn't stopped talking since leaving Havenworth. He wasn't tensely quiet the way he always had been after an encounter with Mr. Bentford. That boded well for his afternoon at Havenworth. It seemed, at the very least, he hadn't been mistreated. Clara felt immense and immediate relief at that.

"Did you know a pony isn't just a baby horse?" Edmund said. "It is different from a horse. It's smaller and has shorter legs and doesn't get bigger when it grows up."

"Is that so?" She'd never heard Edmund talk so much at once.

He slipped his hand inside hers. "And you can brush harder than you think, Aunt Clara. It doesn't hurt them."

"You seem to have learned a great deal."

"I didn't get to ride yet. Mr. Jonquil says I need to be comfortable with horses first. He knows everything about horses."

"Did you spend very much time with Mr. Jonquil?" Clara asked, surprised to hear that Havenworth's owner had been involved in Edmund's chores. If he disapproved of a nonentity of a widow, he would certainly not lower himself to spend time with her ward.

"The whole afternoon. He showed me the stables. They're big as our whole house. There are more than twenty horses. More than thirty, maybe. He knows all of their names. And there are boys in the stable who are only a little older than me. Mr. Jonquil says he started working in the stables when he was too young to even remember. And he says a gentleman can raise horses."

"He is correct about that." Clara loved Edmund's sudden chattiness. She couldn't remember the last time he'd been so cheerful.

"I am to go back on Monday," Edmund continued. "But he said I cannot come to the stables unless I have finished all my lessons and only if you say I have finished my chores at home."

"Did he?" That was thoughtful, at least.

"And he said if I sneak there without permission or don't finish everything at home, I won't be allowed to come for a few days until I learn that a gentleman never neglects his home or his family."

Clara actually stopped in the middle of the lane and stared at Edmund in astonishment. "He said that?" It had always been her experience that the only thing a man never neglected was his own comfort and pleasure.

But Edmund nodded, confirming his tale. The warning didn't seem to have frightened him. Mr. Jonquil must not have taken a threatening or overpowering approach to laying down the rules. Odd, that.

"Is he correct?" Edmund asked, apparently noticing the confusion on her face. "About a gentleman taking care of his family?"

She fumbled for only a moment. "Yes. He is." Whether or not true gentlemen actually did take that approach was irrelevant. She fully meant to raise Edmund so that when he was grown, *he* would treat his family that way.

"I thought so," Edmund said.

They continued their walk, Edmund's tongue never slowing. Clara only half listened. What was Mr. Jonquil about? He obviously didn't think highly of her. She, he had made clear enough through his actions and pointed silences, was beneath his notice. But he'd given Edmund some very sound advice and had shown him around the stables, watching out for the boy.

What was his motive? She'd known enough men in her life to know there was always an ulterior motive.

She sent Edmund up to his bedchamber to wash up and settled herself at her small writing desk in the sitting room. Suzie had returned from Grompton with a letter in the moments before Clara had been obligated to go fetch Edmund. The letter had come from London, and she hadn't opened it before she left. She had but one correspondent in Town, the man of business she'd secured in the days before fleeing Sussex.

Clara held the unopened letter between her hands now. A heaviness settled in her stomach at the memory of that desperate flight. She'd tried so hard to appear calm and unconcerned for the children's sake. But she couldn't remember ever being so afraid in all her life. Her welfare had depended on escaping Bentford Manor. More importantly, however, the children were no longer safe there. If she'd had to decide between sending them away and escaping herself, she would have sent them anywhere she possibly could.

She pushed aside the painful reminders of her past and broke the wax seal on the letter. It was, indeed, from her man of business, Mr. Clark.

Mrs. Bentford,

I fear I have less than satisfactory news regarding your quarterly payment. I was able to transfer the payment from the Bentford Estate to an account I have created in your name, including the address misdirection you requested.

Her circumstances required Mr. Clark to conduct her business as unobtrusively as possible. If Clara drew attention to herself and her location, she'd be found. After all the difficulty she'd gone to escaping her life in Sussex, she couldn't bear the thought of being discovered, of being dragged back to the misery she'd run from.

However, this could not be accomplished without the Bentford man of business being aware of the change. I do not believe he knows of your current location, but he has managed to delay the funds transfer. I fear you will not be receiving your usual quarterly payment anytime in the near future.

If you wish, I can have more funds withdrawn from young Mr. Clifton's accounts that you can repay once this latest difficulty has been worked through.

Please advise as to your preferences.

Yours, etc.

Joseph Clark

Clara slumped in her chair. The last thing she wanted was to draw more money out of Edmund's inheritance. It would simply be unfair for Edmund to have to be required to sacrifice yet again for her.

Now what do I do? We must have money to live on.

Clara refused to crumble under the weight of difficulties. She was no longer the frightened girl she'd been when her father had married her off to a horrid and frightening man. She had found strength and courage in herself that she'd never realized was there. Life was hard, but she was strong.

She pulled a fresh sheet of parchment from her desk and dipped her quill in the inkwell.

Mr. Clark,

Thank you for your efforts on our behalf. I dislike severely the idea of pulling more money from Edmund's account. But neither can I live without money to feed myself and my children.

I am not certain which course of action I ought to take, so I will instead explain my wishes and give you leave to take whichever approach is most likely to achieve that end. I have but two goals, Mr. Clark. The first, that my children have food to eat and a roof over their heads. The second, equally as imperative, perhaps even more so, that Mr. Bentford not find us here.

Please proceed according to your best judgment.

Yours, etc.

Clara Bentford

She sanded the letter and leaned back in her chair. Though she was courageous and determined, she was also painfully aware of the perilous nature of her current situation. The peace and freedom she and the children enjoyed was precarious at best. Everything she had worked for would disappear if Mr. Bentford found them.

Chapter Eight

"MR. JONQUIL TALKED TO JOHNNY real quiet," Edmund said nearly two weeks after he'd first begun his daily trips to Havenworth. "I didn't hear what he said. But Johnny looked real ashamed, like he'd done something he wasn't supposed to. Then Johnny started walking up to the house, and Mr. Jonquil told him that he would ask Fanny—I don't know who that is—if Johnny had apologized to her, so he had better make sure he did."

"Why was Johnny apologizing?" Clara asked. Johnny was the stable hand who brought Edmund home each afternoon. Fanny must have been one of the Havenworth maids.

"Jim said Johnny was playing with Fanny's heart." A look of profound confusion crossed Edmund's face. "I have been trying to figure out what that means."

Edmund looked up to Johnny, spoke of him almost as often as he spoke of Mr. Jonquil. Clara saw no need to discredit a young man who was, in all other respects, a good example to Edmund.

"Jim says Mr. Jonquil doesn't allow any of them to 'mistreat females.'" Edmund spoke the last two words as if quoting verbatim. "And that if he hears they have, he's 'like to tan their hide.'"

"For mistreating a woman?" Clara asked in stunned disbelief.

Edmund shrugged and made a face that indicated he didn't understand the odd behavior either.

"Mr. Jonquil says that being mean to a girl is worse than being mean to a boy." Edmund dropped into a chair in the sitting room. He always returned from Havenworth physically spent. "He said that I should always be kind to you and Alice. He said I wouldn't be a gentleman if I wasn't."

She sat near him, attempting to formulate a reply.

"I told him Mr. Bentford wasn't nice to you and Alice," Edmund said.

"You told him that?" she blurted, inexplicably embarrassed that Mr. Jonquil should know such details about her history.

"So I asked him if Mr. Bentford was a gentleman," Edmund continued, oblivious to her discomfort. "And Mr. Jonquil said if he wasn't nice to you and Alice, then he was 'no kind of a gentleman at all.'"

Clara leaned back in her chair. She didn't know what to make of Mr. Jonquil at all. He seemed too good to be true.

"I think he's right," Edmund said after a silent moment had passed. "I like Mr. Jonquil better than I liked Mr. Bentford."

Clara surprised even herself by saying, "So do I." She realized with a start that she meant it. Granted, there were few people she didn't like better than Mr. Bentford. Mr. Jonquil was kind to Edmund, a point decidedly in his favor.

"Aunt Clara?" Edmund moved to stand beside her chair.

She knew what he wanted. He'd sat on her lap regularly in the three years since he'd come to live with her. Edmund seemed to need the reassurance. Clara held her arms out to him, and Edmund climbed onto her lap.

Suzie brought Alice into the sitting room in the next moment, still sleepy and rubbing her eyes.

Alice spotted Edmund cuddled on Clara's lap. "Me too, Mama?"

Clara nodded, grateful the chair was a sturdy one. Alice toddled to Clara's knee and made a valiant effort to climb onto her lap but found her legs unequal to the height. Before Clara had a chance to so much as adjust her position, Edmund reached his hand down to Alice and helped her climb up.

Edmund had always been a good boy, but Clara had never seen him offer Alice his assistance without being prompted.

"I'm a gentleman," Edmund softly declared, leaning against Clara once more.

"Yes, you are." Clara silently thanked the heavens for Mr. Jonquil's influence on the boy. She couldn't approve of the man himself, knowing he so wholeheartedly disapproved of her. But he at least seemed to be a good influence. She would give him credit for that much.

Clara heard the sound of approaching horse hooves. Edmund obviously did as well.

"It's Mr. Jonquil!" he declared, scrambling down.

Alice wasn't so quick, so Clara swung her into her arms. "Edmund, we don't know who it is," she warned, trying to stop him from opening the door. What if Mr. Bentford had found them? What if *he* was standing on the other side? That question plagued her every single time they had a visitor.

But she wasn't fast enough to prevent Edmund from pulling the door open. His face fell, and Clara's heart dropped to her feet. She reached for Edmund. But the man who stepped inside was not the man she'd feared to find there. It was Mr. Finley.

He was in the sitting room in the next moment, slipping inside the house as smoothly as a snake. "Mrs. Bentford," he greeted and bowed.

She did not like Mr. Finley, didn't remotely trust him. She stood as firmly and calmly as she could manage, setting Alice on the floor beside her. Edmund took Alice by the hand. Did he feel as uneasy with Mr. Finley as she did? She gently nudged the children behind her.

"Is there a particular reason for your visit, Mr. Finley?" Clara used the tone of neutrality she had perfected in response to Mr. Bentford's repeated attacks.

"I happened to be riding past and wished to offer you good day," Mr. Finley said. His drawl had grated on her from their very first meeting. He made her feel like an object he was assessing rather than a person he was speaking with.

But she was no longer intimidated by such behavior. Life had taught her to stand up for herself and to defend her children. "Finley Grange is on the other side of Grompton, at least three-quarters of an hour by horseback," she said confidently. "I daresay most of your business is conducted in Collingham."

"Ah, but I had business at Havenworth, my dear Mrs. Bentford. In order to reach there, I must pass by here."

"On the contrary, you must pass Havenworth to reach Ivy Cottage." Clara kept perfectly calm despite the worrisome situation. She had only ever faced down Mr. Finley while in the company of other people. He felt more threatening when she was so alone. She refused to break down, refused to once again be a victim too afraid to defend herself.

"But it was near enough that I simply could not allow the opportunity to slip by." He was clearly losing patience with her. Though his smile didn't slip, something hardened in his eyes. He obviously expected her to be flattered that a man of his standing had noticed a woman of her poverty.

Clara was instantly on alert. She had not a single servant at hand, no male relative to force Mr. Finley from the property. She was vulnerable, and she suspected Mr. Finley knew that. Her only course of action was to counteract that appearance.

"Well, you have offered your good day, so do not let me detain you from your pressing business," Clara said forcefully. She would show no weakness.

"I have a few moments." Mr. Finley stepped closer to her. He reached out his hand, clearly meaning to touch her.

She stepped backward. She needed the presence of another person, one over the age of seven. "Edmund, go get Suzie," she whispered to Edmund. He obediently hurried from the room.

"Mama," Alice whimpered, tugging on Clara's hand.

Clara gently shushed her.

"She looks a great deal like you," Mr. Finley observed. "A beautiful child."

"Thank you, sir." Clara made no move to sit or to offer him a chair. Where was Suzie?

"Come now, Mrs. Bentford." Mr. Finley smiled artfully at her. "Can we not sit and enjoy a cup of tea? Perhaps we might discuss the fine weather we have been enjoying."

"I do not entertain callers on Fridays, Mr. Finley." She allowed a reprimand to tint her words.

"You must grow lonely"—Mr. Finley moved closer still—"without a single soul coming to call all the day long."

His observation felt like a threat, as if he meant to remind her of her isolated and unprotected state.

"Your concern is appreciated," Clara lied, "but I assure you I am quite content."

"My dear," Mr. Finley said, moving forward. Little more than a foot remained between them. "I would have you more than content. I would wish for you to be joyously happy."

Even his *joyously happy* sounded ominous. Clara was pressed against the back of the sofa with no way to maneuver around Mr. Finley. He stood too close and appeared far too satisfied with the arrangement.

The door opened. Clara's heart thudded ever harder. Edmund took a single step inside, clutching Mr. Jonquil's sleeve, his countenance tight and worried.

"Mr. Jonquil." Clara hoped she sounded welcoming. She attempted to slip around Mr. Finley, who was quite effectively blocking her path. Mr. Jonquil was far preferable to Mr. Finley, even if he looked as disapproving as ever. "Do come in."

"I was—I have a book. For Edmund." Mr. Jonquil's eyes darted between her and Mr. Finley.

"He promised to bring it," Edmund quietly explained.

Clara glanced quickly at the book in Edmund's hand.

"Mister!" Alice recognized their visitor quite suddenly. She bolted from Clara's side and threw her arms around Mr. Jonquil's right leg.

"Alice," Mr. Jonquil quietly greeted, gently patting Alice's head.

"Will you not come sit for a while?" Clara offered. *Please stay,* she silently pleaded. She was willing to fight for herself and the children but knew Mr. Jonquil's presence would make that far easier. Mr. Finley was already less discomforting.

"I cannot stay." Mr. Jonquil's eyes settled on Mr. Finley, his expression unreadable.

"A moment at least?" she pressed. *Please.*

Mr. Jonquil shook his head, his mouth set in a tight line.

"Havenworth," Clara blurted. "Mr. Finley was only just saying he has business at Havenworth. Indeed, he told me that was the very reason he was in the neighborhood."

Mr. Finley finally turned to Mr. Jonquil. They offered curt bows.

"Finley," Mr. Jonquil acknowledged the other man.

"Jonquil," was the equally ungallant reply.

Clara slipped out of reach while Mr. Finley was distracted.

"What business do you have at Havenworth?" Mr. Jonquil asked quietly.

"Rumor has it Lord Cavratt will be descending on you shortly," Mr. Finley said, with something like a smirk on his face. "Coming to look over the animals to be auctioned in a few months' time."

Mr. Jonquil's nod seemed reluctant.

"I understand a brother or two will also be arriving," Mr. Finley added. "As I am considering purchasing a pair for my phaeton, I thought I should have a peek myself."

"You can look," Mr. Jonquil replied calmly. "But . . . but I decide who buys."

"Still harboring a little resentment, Jonquil?" Mr. Finley chuckled menacingly as he made his way closer to the doorway. He turned, a foot or two from Mr. Jonquil, and looked back at Clara. "Good day, my dear," he offered with a sweeping bow.

The two gentleman bumped shoulders as Mr. Finley passed through the doorway. Mr. Jonquil did not budge. He looked angry. Outside, horse's hooves clattered away from the cottage. Clara breathed easier. Mr. Finley was gone.

Mr. Jonquil, however, was not. He watched her quite closely, his gaze never wavering. She could think of nothing to say. Why did he look disappointed beneath his stern expression? And why did she feel guilty being the recipient of such a look? She'd done nothing wrong. Indeed, she'd defended herself against an ill-meaning man. She'd stood her ground. She had effectively sent Mr. Finley off.

After a moment, Mr. Jonquil bowed quite properly, though not as elegantly as Mr. Finley had. Clara thought she heard a "Good day."

"And to you, Mr. Jonquil," Clara managed, fighting a sudden urge to tear up. It was a completely illogical reaction but was forceful enough that she could not ignore it.

What was happening to her? She had always been levelheaded. She never cried without reason, never found her emotions rising to the surface without warning. The past six months she had been stronger than in all the twenty-two years before that. Why was she crumbling now?

"I will see you tomorrow, Mr. Jonquil," Edmund said anxiously. Mr. Jonquil nodded at him and ruffled the boy's hair.

"Mister!" Alice called out to him, arms outstretched.

He paused long enough to hunch down and kiss the top of her head before turning and walking away. The kindness of that gesture momentarily captured Clara's entire attention.

Mr. Finley's exit had brought immediate, palpable relief. For reasons Clara could not begin to understand, seeing Mr. Jonquil go—Mr. Jonquil, who seemed to perpetually disapprove of her, who seemed ever eager to be out of her company—did not bring any relief, only a growing sense of confusion.

Chapter Nine

Finley. Why was it always Finley?

The only scuffle Corbin had had at Eton had been with Finley. Stanley, Corbin's younger brother, now a captain with the Thirteenth Light Dragoons, had been in his first year at school and was suffering through a severe bout of homesickness. Finley and a few other boys several years older than Corbin had found Stanley's dejection quite humorous and had joined forces to make him as miserable as possible.

In the end, Corbin probably wouldn't have been sent down over the fight that had ensued if he hadn't dropped four of them, including Finley, who'd come out of the ordeal with a bloodied but not-quite-broken nose. Corbin had made a mess of the entire group of bullies, a use of force the headmaster had deemed "a bit excessive."

Corbin had expected a severe dressing down from Father. "You must have been severely provoked," Father had said as they'd walked along the River Trent during Corbin's fortnight of banishment at home. "What did they do?"

"They hurt Stanley."

"Stanley needs to learn to fight his own battles," Father said.

Corbin clamped down his disappointment and nodded.

"So give him a few pointers when you get back, will you?"

Corbin looked up at Father then and saw him grinning. He smiled back.

"Dropped four of them, did you?" Father nodded his head in a way that spoke of pride.

"It felt good," Corbin answered.

Father laughed out loud and ruffled his hair. They spent the next half hour talking over the skirmish. Father offered some advice and taught

Corbin a few of the finer points of pugilism. It was one of Corbin's fondest memories. Father lived only another four years.

Finley kept his distance from Corbin for some time after their skirmish, though he taunted him ceaselessly. Anytime Corbin found himself in an embarrassing situation, Finley seemed to be there.

Philip and Layton, the two oldest Jonquils, and Crispin Handle, who'd been like another Jonquil from the time he and Philip had met at Eton, had realized Finley's personal vendetta against Corbin, and a year almost to the day after that bloody fistfight, they'd somehow managed to remove every pair of trousers and underclothes from Finley's room. Seeing George Finley roaring mad, his chicken-thin legs exposed beneath his barely long-enough shirt, had been one of the finer moments of Corbin's educational experience.

From that point on, Finley and the Jonquils, including Crispin, had been rivals.

Now Finley was after Clara. If the scene Corbin had stumbled on at Ivy Cottage the evening before was any indication, Finley was making far more progress than he was.

My dear. He'd called her *my dear.* And she hadn't corrected him.

Clara couldn't possibly know what Finley was truly like. Her late husband—if Edmund's account was accurate, and Corbin felt certain it was—had been boorish and unkind and, though Edmund hadn't said as much, Corbin suspected the man had been abusive as well, with his words and his hands.

Finley would be no better. He was arrogant to the point of being dangerous. So sure was he that he deserved to be given anything he demanded that he lashed out when denied. Women were his targets more often than not. Perhaps because they were inherently more vulnerable. The law, society, the indifference of far too many men, all conspired to leave too many women unprotected and undervalued.

Corbin didn't know what to do. Even if Clara had no interest in *him,* she deserved far better than Finley.

"Vis'tors." Jim interrupted Corbin's thoughts.

Corbin looked up. Two coaches sat under the portico. He'd been expecting Crispin and Catherine and recognized the Cavratt crest emblazoned on the side of one of the coaches. The other coach was one of the unmarked carriages from the Lampton stables—Corbin had spent so much time in those stables he recognized each of the equipages on sight.

Had Mater come as well? If she had, Charlie, the youngest Jonquil at only seventeen, would be with her, as would Caroline, Corbin's little niece. If Mater had traveled from the Park, it could only mean one thing: Charlie had managed to get himself in trouble. Philip had left Corbin in charge for just that reason. Charlie was always in trouble.

Simmons looked pleased when Corbin reached the front doors of Havenworth. They seldom had visitors—having people around made Corbin nervous. His unease was a little less pronounced with his family. And, he realized with a smile, with Edmund. He enjoyed the boy tremendously.

"The Dowager Lady Lampton, Lord and Lady Cavratt, Mr. Jason Jonquil, Mr. Harold Jonquil, Mr. Charles Jonquil, and Miss Caroline Jonquil." Simmons quickly rattled off the list of arrivals. Ever since coming to Havenworth, Simmons had made a practice of warning Corbin of any and all visitors. Corbin hadn't needed to ask him to; Simmons simply seemed to understand.

It was something of a family reunion. Even Harry had come. Corbin nodded to Simmons and swiftly walked to the sitting room.

"Good day, dear." Mater greeted him with an affectionate kiss on the cheek. "Forgive us for descending on you without warning, but if we had remained at the Park one day longer, I would probably have killed your brother."

She smiled as if sincere. Corbin glanced across at Charlie, who sat slouched in a chair at the far end of the room. Corbin looked back at Mater, allowing a question to enter his eyes.

Mater seemed to understand the unspoken "What did Charlie do this time?"

"He took Philip's phaeton at an unnatural pace down the lane outside Squire Hampton's home," she explained. "Only by some miracle, he managed not to run Arabella Hampton down, though he positively ruined her gown."

"I didn't know it was muddy," Corbin thought he heard Charlie grumble.

"And last week he wasted an entire afternoon strutting like a peacock around Collingham," Mater continued. "I have not yet stopped hearing how ridiculous he was."

Charlie always seemed to be in some scrape or another when at home. He'd been nearly perfectly behaved during their Christmas holiday in Suffolk. Corbin had never heard a word about trouble at school. But at home, it was an entirely different story. Why was that?

"I had hoped we might remain until the workers finished remodeling the dower house," Mater said. "That might mean a fortnight or more."

"Of course." Corbin always enjoyed having his mother visit.

"Harold is only here for the day," Mater volunteered. "He has a sermon in the morning."

Harold nodded quite seriously, wearing the pious look on his face that always indicated he was pondering something of deep, doctrinal significance. If not for the fact that he wore that look most of the time, Corbin might have found it a reliable measure of Harold's thoughts.

"Uncle Corbo?" A little voice captured his attention.

He looked down into the face of a golden-haired angel, her bright blue eyes wide and inquiring and, to his instant dismay, teary. He scooped his little niece into his arms.

She laid her head on his shoulder. "When is my papa coming home?"

Her father and his new wife were on an extended wedding trip. "In another week, Caroline," Corbin answered.

Mater smiled at the two of them and crossed the room to sit on a sofa. She was probably quite worn out with the energetic five-year-old at the house, not to mention enduring Charlie's often-embarrassing escapades.

"And Mary will come back too?" Caroline inquired after her new stepmother, whose name was actually Marion.

She will come home with your papa. Corbin nodded.

"If we write them a letter, will they come home sooner?"

Corbin smiled. "Are . . . are you unhappy? Grammy and Uncle Charming aren't . . . aren't keeping you company?" Caroline had rather amusing names for all of her relatives. Philip's wife, Sorrel, had become "Swirl." Corbin wondered what name Caroline would craft for Clara, given the chance.

"Charming is never at home, and Grammy gets tired."

A bolt of inspiration hit at that moment. "Two of my neighbors are children," Corbin whispered to Caroline. "Would you like to meet them?"

"Oh, Uncle Corbo!" She squeezed his neck tighter. "No one plays with me anymore. Mary just wants to be with Papa. And I want to have friends to play with."

"I will write to"—*Clara*—"their mother."

"Thank you." Caroline grinned. "You're the best uncle in the whole world!"

"That is a rather bold declaration for a young lady with seven uncles," Corbin's twin, Jason, said from nearby, a chuckle in his tone. *Seven* included

Crispin, Lord Cavratt. "Aren't I your favorite uncle?" Jason smiled at Caroline.

"You're my favorite uncle in London," Caroline clarified quite matter-of-factly.

"I suppose I'll have to be satisfied with that." Jason shrugged. "How are you, Corbin?"

Corbin nodded, his usual response to most questions.

"What did you do to earn the title of favorite uncle?" Jason asked when Caroline abandoned them and skipped across the room to where Crispin and his wife, Catherine, were engaged in a private conversation.

"Invited children."

"For her to play with," Jason finished the thought. They'd been able to do that all their lives, communicate without actually speaking to each other. It had been convenient for Corbin, who preferred not talking. "Genius. The only thing I brought from London was a bag of toffee and a monumental headache."

Corbin looked at his twin. They weren't identical but, as Jonquils, looked alike. The headache, Corbin knew instinctively, was not illness-induced but was brought on by tension. "Difficult case?" he asked. Jason was a barrister.

"A difficult client," Jason muttered, obvious disapproval and annoyance on his face. But in his eyes, there was also frustration of a different type.

"Is she?" Corbin asked.

"Despite the fact that I am her legal counsel, Miss Thornton is convinced she knows better than I do on every matter. She descends on my office unannounced and expects immediate and undivided attention. She is a harpy of the first order, but my secretary as well as every other barrister in the entire building is practically falling at her feet. And—" Jason stopped abruptly. "How did you know this client was a she?"

Corbin just smiled.

"Are you dealing with a difficult woman too, Corbin?" Jason asked, a little amusement sneaking across his face.

"Not difficult. Just—"

"Elusive," Jason finished for him.

Corbin nodded.

"Is she a harpy?" Jason asked as if warning him.

Corbin shook his head no.

"Does she order you around?"

Corbin chuckled and shook his head again.

Jason nodded his approval. "You're having trouble winning her over?"

"She doesn't notice me." *At all.*

Jason's look became quite knowing. "That's your problem. You have to make an impression."

Corbin sighed. "Philip said . . ." He finished with a nod, knowing Jason would understand what he meant to say.

"You haven't been listening to Philip, have you? He probably told you to dress like a fop and simper about." Jason shook his head. "No lady is interested in a gentleman who wears brighter colors than she does."

It hadn't gone well, that was for sure and certain. Corbin had yet to determine a better approach for capturing Clara's attention. He'd summoned the courage to go to Ivy Cottage the day before, hoping he could at least manage a somewhat sensible conversation. But Finley had already been there.

"I will tell you what you need to do," Jason began, but Crispin interrupted in the next moment.

"Is there time to go down to the stables today, Corbin?" he asked, an eagerness in his tone that Corbin had never heard.

"Crispin," Catherine lightly scolded.

Corbin nodded. "The mare you asked about is there."

"Good. Good. And I need to look over your ponies as well."

Ponies? What need did Crispin have for a pony?

"Crispin." Catherine repeated her plea. This time her face had pinked with obvious embarrassment.

"Catherine." Crispin turned back to her. "We will have to have a pony."

"But not immediately," she whispered, her color intensifying.

"How soon do you need it? The pony?"

"In the fall," Crispin answered without hesitation.

"Crispin." The plea had turned almost frantic.

A piece of the puzzle fell quite suddenly into place. Ponies were for children. Crispin and Catherine were, apparently, expecting the first addition to their family.

"Catherine, we have to have a pony," Crispin replied a touch impatiently.

Catherine's eyes quickly scanned the assembly, all of whom watched the exchange with obvious interest. The color in her cheeks reached a rosy-red hue, and tears seemed to threaten in her eyes. A quiver of her chin was the only warning before she fled at a run from the room.

"Now what did I do?" Crispin muttered to himself.

"Embarrassed her," Corbin offered quietly.

"You essentially announced her condition," Jason added with a raised eyebrow.

"I guess I did do that, didn't I?" Crispin sighed. "Excuse me," he offered to the room at large. "I need to go apologize to my wife. Again."

"When can I meet my friends?" Caroline asked into the silence after Crispin left.

"I'll write now."

Caroline smiled in reply.

Corbin sat at the writing desk, quill in hand but mind too busy for writing. If he invited Clara's children to Havenworth, would she come as well? He hoped she would.

What if she came and was completely oblivious to his presence? Three of his brothers, Crispin and Catherine, and Mater were all at Havenworth. Corbin would be overlooked in that crowd, as always. Or suppose Clara spent the visit talking of Finley? Being passed over for that parasite of a man would be torturous.

What if she disapproved of his family? What if his family disapproved of her? What if he made a fool of himself again?

Corbin shook his head and dipped his quill in the inkwell. He'd promised Caroline. Corbin didn't break his promises.

Chapter Ten

Mrs. Bentford,

Please excuse my presumption in writing to you, but I must beg a favor.

Clara let her eyes slip to the signature at the bottom of the page. *Mr. Corbin Jonquil.* A favor?

My niece, who is five years old, has come to Havenworth for a visit and is wishing for the company of other children. I had hoped you might consent to allow Edmund and Alice to come to Havenworth this afternoon at two of the clock for tea in the nursery and to meet Caroline. I assure you she is a well-behaved girl.

If, however, this is not to your liking or convenience, I will, of course, understand and shall remain,

Yours, etc.

Mr. Corbin Jonquil

Mr. Jonquil's Christian name suited him. It was unique but not in an obvious way. She liked it very much. Very much indeed. Clara stopped short. That was a tangent she hadn't anticipated her thoughts following.

She shook off the distraction and forced herself to focus on the request Mr. Jonquil had made.

Tea in the nursery. It seemed a very formal affair for children. Alice was only two years old and would most likely spend the afternoon amused at how nicely her fist fit in her teacup. Was Mr. Jonquil's niece the daughter of the earl? He had not referred to her as *Lady* Caroline, though that might be more a reflection of their closeness than an indication that she did not possess the title. The young lady would likely be appalled at Alice's lack of refinement. She might even scold the poor girl. Not that Alice would mind—she wouldn't even understand. But Edmund would. He was a sensitive boy and would be hurt by the reprimand, even if not aimed at himself.

Clara glanced across the meadow at Edmund, who was playing bowls quite contentedly on his own. Only two weeks earlier Clara would have been hard-pressed to urge the boy out of doors.

"A man needs fresh air, Aunt Clara," Edmund had told her one afternoon after returning from Havenworth. He said it with that air of authority Clara had come to realize always accompanied a piece of wisdom told him by Mr. Jonquil, whom Edmund declared knew *everything*. Ever since that day, Edmund had spent time, without Clara's insistence, out of doors: running, playing, occasionally just lying on his back in the grass, watching the clouds.

He was like a new boy, confident in ways she never would have imagined, though still quiet and shy. He had already grown healthier, his bony frame filling out from exertion and activity. His appetite had increased to unparalleled levels. It was a very good thing they weren't teetering on the edge of poverty, or Edmund would be eating them out of house and home.

He smiled more. That was the very best change of all. When she'd asked Mr. Jonquil to take Edmund on, Clara had hoped simply to give Edmund something to look forward to each day. She hadn't anticipated the influence Mr. Jonquil would have on him.

Clara looked back at the letter in her hands. Mr. Jonquil really hadn't asked much, a simple visit. She could accompany the children, see to it that they were well received.

"If the atmosphere at Havenworth is too cold, we can always leave," Clara told herself. Despite her well-crafted scheme and her determination to remain out of Mr. Jonquil's debt in the matter of the horses, Clara found herself very much indebted. Bringing the children to spend an afternoon with Mr. Jonquil's niece was not much of a sacrifice when weighed against all he'd done for Edmund.

A man who was a good influence? Clara shook her head in disbelief. It had never before seemed possible. And yet, having found someone who seemed to be exactly that, she found she couldn't walk away without learning more about him.

* * *

"I want to go home, Aunt Clara," Edmund whimpered.

Clara secretly agreed. All her bravado had faded during the walk over. There was every possibility that more than one member of the aristocracy had come to visit Havenworth. The prospect was astoundingly intimidating. Voices echoed from up ahead. Clara had a feeling they were about to face more than just a five-year-old girl.

The butler led them into what Clara assumed was the drawing room. She grasped Edmund's and Alice's hands. They could survive a room full of lofty people—they'd certainly survived worse.

"Mrs. Bentford. Mr. Edmund Clifton. Miss Alice Bentford." After making his announcement, the butler stepped aside.

Edmund's hand tightened around Clara's. A sea of faces watched them enter. Clara froze. The room was full of men. Tea in the nursery, the invitation had said. Mr. Jonquil had mentioned nothing about a house full of tall, fully grown men. She glanced around quickly, immediately and entirely on her guard. Then looked again, amazed.

The men quite closely resembled Mr. Jonquil: golden hair, blue eyes, and tall, lean builds. The similarities were pronounced enough to be almost eerie.

"Mister!" Alice shrieked excitedly. How could the girl tell which one was which? Alice ran to the side where Clara hadn't been looking and threw herself at Mr. Jonquil as she always did.

He didn't hesitate but scooped her off the floor and into his arms. "I've found you a friend, Alice."

She simply repeated her earlier squeal and squirmed in his arms, squeezing his neck ever harder. Mr. Jonquil smiled at Alice, and Clara felt herself relax. He was different somehow than she'd seen him before, more at ease. But, then, he was among his peers, she would guess, looking around at the fine clothing in the room.

Edmund had tucked himself quite firmly out of view behind her skirts. He kept himself hidden, even as Mr. Jonquil came up next to them.

"I'm afraid Edmund is having second thoughts," Clara whispered to Mr. Jonquil, not wanting to embarrass the boy but wishing to explain and, hopefully, avoid any humiliation Edmund might suffer should those gathered be inconsiderate.

Mr. Jonquil seemed to study her for a moment. Clara fidgeted a little under the scrutiny. Did he realize she too was doubting the wisdom of this visit?

He nodded, then turned to Edmund. "May I introduce you to my brothers?" Clara heard him say softly to the white-faced boy.

"I suppose," Edmund whispered, his voice shaking a little.

Had she been wrong to come? Edmund always felt uneasy in social situations.

"Mr. Clifton." Mr. Jonquil spoke quite formally, turning a little to face the room. Alice continued to cling to his neck. "May I introduce you to Mr. Jonquil." He motioned at one of his look-alikes. "Mr. Jonquil." He gestured to another. "And Mr. Jonquil."

Edmund snickered. Clara couldn't keep back a smile.

"Don't laugh, you'll forget . . . won't remember their names," Mr. Jonquil warned.

At that, Edmund laughed harder. Clara watched as he slipped his hand in Mr. Jonquil's. No, that would no longer suffice; the room held far too many Mr. Jonquils. *Corbin*, she reminded herself. Their Mr. Jonquil was named Corbin.

Their Mr. Jonquil? Clara forced that uncomfortable thought to the back of her mind.

"This"—Corbin indicated the Mr. Jonquil who seemed nearest to his own age and resembled him most closely—"is Jason. He is a barrister. We are twins."

Twins? Despite the remarkable family resemblance, Clara did not think they were identical as some twins were. Edmund seemed impressed by the connection, just the same. He nodded his understanding and simply stared at the man.

"This"—Corbin moved to the Mr. Jonquil who wore an extremely sober expression, matched by the black he wore from head to toe, except for the white of his cravat and collar—"is Harold. He's a vicar."

Clara nodded even as Edmund did. The gentleman's occupation explained his sobriety.

"And Charlie." Corbin motioned to a youth with the same golden hair and blue eyes and familiarly featured face. "He just finished at Eton."

A *young* man, then.

"My Aunt Clara says I will go to Eton next year." Edmund's voluntary response shocked Clara to the very soles of her feet. Edmund never spoke of his own volition to strangers.

Charlie smiled in return. "Next year, is it?" he asked.

Edmund nodded, eyes wide.

Charlie looked at Corbin. "We'll have to introduce him to Fennel Kendrick. Never hurts to have someone there looking out for a new boy."

Who was this Fennel Kendrick? Was he trustworthy? Would he look out for Edmund or simply make things worse?

Corbin looked at Clara, almost as if sensing her uncertainty.

"Fennel is a friend of your family's?" she asked.

"He is a fine young man," Corbin said. He offered nothing further, but his words eased her concerns for the present.

Mr. Bentford would have harangued her for her concerns, taunted her with them. *No.* Mr. Bentford would have been oblivious to her concerns, haranguing and taunting her for her deficiencies instead. Having an audience as witness would only have increased the likelihood of a scold.

Corbin Jonquil, she realized, had never belittled her. He had often seemed to look down on her, but he had never humiliated her. He was sweet and patient with her children, holding them quite as if he had been doing so all their lives.

How unexpected—*pleasantly* unexpected for a man.

"Did they come, Uncle Corbo?" a child's voice asked, pulling Clara's attention, and everyone else's, it seemed, to the doorway.

Clara shook her head in amazement as yet another pair of blue eyes and a head of golden hair skipped into the room. This time, however, the golden hair hung in perfect ringlets all around a cherubic face. The child was beautiful.

For a moment, watching the little girl, Clara mourned for the child she had once been. Unlike this angelic girl, Clara had always worn long sleeves to cover the bruises there. She had kept to corners, afraid of her own shadow, watching the people around her with an inescapable feeling of terror. Nothing showed in this girl's face but curiosity.

"Caroline," Corbin greeted the tiny angel. "May I . . . This is Edmund Clifton."

Caroline curtsied prettily. If she wasn't the daughter of an earl, she certainly had the air of one. Edmund hid himself behind Corbin.

"And this"—Corbin bounced Alice as she clung on his neck—"is Alice Bentford."

Alice giggled. As always, the sound pulled an answering laugh from Clara.

Corbin looked over, apparently surprised to hear her laugh. Clara was a little surprised as well. Strangely nervous at his sudden gaze, Clara could only manage a smile. She expected him to be dismissive or disapproving of her show of levity. But he surprised her. Corbin smiled back, his gaze lingering on her.

"Do you like dolls?" she heard Caroline ask.

She assumed the question was directed at Alice. But it was Edmund who answered. "No," he quite adamantly declared.

Clara held back a laugh, not wanting to embarrass Edmund. He was doing better than usual with strangers.

"Do you like cake?" Caroline tried again.

"Mm-hmm."

Clara's eyes darted to Corbin. He seemed to be enjoying the children's conversation as much as she was. She felt an unexpected kinship with him.

"There is cake in the nursery." Caroline shared the information with Edmund, almost as if it was a closely guarded secret. Edmund smiled a little. "And biscuits."

"Biscuits!" Alice squealed and began wiggling out of Corbin's arms.

Caroline clapped her hands together as if thoroughly delighted. A young woman, whom Clara assumed was the nursemaid, led the children from the room. Edmund lagged a little behind but followed without any prodding from Clara.

Corbin chuckled lightly. "How quickly she abandoned me."

"There are few things Alice likes better than biscuits," Clara said.

The smile remained on his lips. Clara turned back, as he did, toward the room. Her own smile vanished in an instant.

A lady of indeterminate years, quite finely attired with crystal-blue eyes that seemed far too insightful, looked directly at Clara. She didn't appear pleased—confused, perhaps. The lady's gaze moved from Corbin to Clara and back again, her expression never clearing.

Clara stood her ground, though she very much felt like fleeing. Every eye in the room was on her, confusion written on every face.

"Mater," Corbin interrupted the silence, "this is . . . May I introduce Mrs. Bentford. Mrs. Bentford, this is my mother, the Dowager Countess of Lampton."

Clara offered her best curtsy. *A countess? I must be utterly insignificant to her.*

"Mrs. Bentford," Corbin continued, "may I intro . . . This is . . . I—"

He stopped. Clara heard him take a breath, then watched as he muttered silently. She couldn't make out his grumblings. After a moment, he continued with the introductions.

"This is Mr. Jason Jonquil, Mr. Harold Jonquil, and Mr. Charlie Jonquil," he said very quickly. To his brothers, Corbin said, "This is Mrs. Bentford."

Never before had she been so grateful that her governess had insisted she learn to curtsy properly. Clara would make certain Alice learned as well.

"Mrs. Bentford." The dowager countess addressed her, still something like shock lingering on her face. "Do you live in the neighborhood?"

"Yes, Lady Lampton," Clara answered as composed as she could manage to be. She would give the countess no reason to disapprove of her manners. "I believe we are your son's nearest neighbors."

"In the cottage? Just west of here?" the dowager pressed.

"Yes." Clara did not like that all eyes in the room were trained on her. Three men. Four if she counted Corbin, though he did not make her nervous the way the others did.

"And *Mr.* Bentford?" the dowager pressed.

"Mater," Corbin quietly interrupted, "Mrs. Bentford is . . . She is a widow."

"A widow," the dowager repeated in an amazed whisper.

Clara glanced around. Smiles had spread across the faces of all three Jonquil brothers. Corbin had turned a little red. Why did Clara have the feeling she'd missed something?

"Have you been in the neighborhood long?" Jason—Clara felt nearly certain that was the barrister's name—asked.

"About six months," Clara answered, feeling herself tense. Had they all moved closer, or did it simply feel that way?

Jason smiled even more broadly. The siblings exchanged a few looks. Corbin remained silent, his color rising. Did her presence embarrass him? The thought settled like a weight on her heart.

"Oh, Mrs. Bentford!" The dowager suddenly seemed emotional. "You're newly arrived. And you're a widow."

Clara took a step back, all her defenses up. Why had that information struck the countess as significant? Heaven help her if the Jonquils had discovered her history. They would likely help Mr. Bentford drag her back to Bentford Manor.

An actual tear shimmered at the corner of the dowager's eye. "This is so . . . so . . ."

Tears? Tears made no sense whatsoever. Something was decidedly wrong, and Clara had no idea what. The dowager seemed not entirely in control of her faculties. The men in the room were unwavering in their attention.

"I really should stay with the children," Clara said rather quickly. "Edmund is uncomfortable with strangers."

With a quick and probably poorly executed curtsy, Clara hurried from the room. She would locate the nursery and make a hasty exit. She didn't know the Jonquils' intentions, but she couldn't feel comfortable among them. They were too pointed in their questioning of her, too far above her in station, and, more to the point, too heavy on males.

Chapter Eleven

MATER WAS TEARY. CORBIN DIDN'T know what had set her off. He had introduced her to Clara and, within a minute's time, Mater had become emotional. At the same time, his brothers had all looked remarkably close to laughing.

It was no wonder Clara had bolted. Corbin had tried to think of the right words to ask her to stay. But she'd been obviously anxious to go.

"So that was the famous widow recently moved into the neighborhood." Jason smiled, taking a seat near Corbin by the windows of the sitting room.

Corbin could only stare in confusion.

Jason shrugged. "Philip wrote and told us."

Philip never had been one for passing up a good story.

"We were informed you had shown an inordinate amount of interest in a widow who had recently come to live near Havenworth. Philip indicated she lived in the cottage just west of your property line." Jason was using his barrister's voice as he rattled off the list of evidence. Corbin very nearly rolled his eyes. "Now a young lady who lives in said cottage arrives, and you, brother, cannot keep your eyes off her for more than a moment. She declares she only just arrived in the neighborhood and is indeed a widow. Hence, Mrs. Bentford is the newly arrived widow of your conversation with Philip."

Very well reasoned, Corbin acknowledged. He sighed in frustration. "She doesn't—"

"Know you exist?" Jason finished for him. "I put that together, that she's the elusive lady you spoke of before."

Illusive, yes. But she'd smiled at him. It had been fleeting, but she'd smiled. She'd been in his house, smiling at him, laughing with him.

"You should have asked her to stay," Jason said.

Corbin nodded. He'd wanted to do just that, but the words would never have come out whole. With his articulate and self-possessed brothers nearby for comparison, he would have made an even worse impression than he no doubt already had.

"You are too passive, Corbin," Jason said. "You have to stand up. Take charge. Be strong. Tough. No lady is going to have any respect for you if you are walked all over."

Strong? Tough? Corbin was physically quite strong—the result of years spent in the stables—but that, he knew, wasn't what Jason meant.

"There is a reason ladies swoon over rogues. They are dominant personalities," Jason said. "And they fall for soldiers because of the powerful image they put out."

Corbin wrinkled his forehead, thinking. It was logical.

Jason seemed to warm to his topic. "A lady wishes for a gentleman to be in command. If you always seem weak, she won't take you seriously."

In command? Dominant personality? Corbin knew he was neither of those things. How did a man go about appearing that way? Corbin remembered watching the Corinthian set around Town. Ladies were constantly swooning over that group of gentlemen.

They swaggered. Not so much a limp but a rhythm to their walk. A strut. They always looked as if they'd only just dismounted or come in from a round of fisticuffs or a quick sword fight somewhere. Perhaps mussed hair would be helpful. And a little dirt.

The Corinthians didn't bother with flashy wardrobes or high shirt points. They looked like sportsmen: rough, powerful, like Jason had said. It was the complete opposite of Philip's advice, which had turned out horribly.

Corbin shook his head. He could never pull it off. The Corinthians were the men-about-Town. He was Corbin Jonquil: the quiet brother, the unobtrusive one, the Jonquil most people didn't realize even existed, the one Mater actually cried to see in the same room as a lady.

That last thought was the clincher. He had to do something before he became entirely pathetic. But what?

He stood near the windows for some time, pondering what he might do, short of another drastic transformation, to catch Clara's eye. She was in his house, after all. When would he have another opportunity like this one?

Harold came and stood beside him at the window. "Mrs. Bentford seems a good sort of lady."

Corbin nodded.

"I cannot help noticing, however"—Harold's brows furrowed in a look that had pegged him as a future vicar from the time he was in leading strings—"that you did not speak much to her."

Corbin raised an eyebrow in vague annoyance.

Harold held up a hand in acknowledgment of the words Corbin left unspoken. "I know you are not generally given to talkativeness. Yet, I feel inclined to offer a word of advice." Harold was most vicarlike in that moment. Thoughts of Philip and Layton calling him "Holy Harry" throughout their childhood nearly brought a smile to Corbin's face. "A lady can learn a great deal about a man through his conversation. His words will reveal the substance of his character. If he is a reliable, stable sort of gentleman, his words will reflect a certain sobriety. If, however, he is a flighty sort, his conversation will tend toward the overly jovial. Without some words spoken between you, Mrs. Bentford will have no knowledge of your character."

Despite the advice coming from his *younger* brother, Corbin felt the words held more than a grain of truth. "You think . . . think I should talk to her?"

Harold nodded ponderously. "Allow her to see who you are through your words."

He might as well have suggested Corbin get up during services on Sunday and dance a jig before the entire congregation. "I'm not good with words."

"I am not suggesting you entertain her with a never-ending string of witticisms or pointless stories." Harold shook his head in a way that put Corbin instantly in mind of the vicar at Lampton Park while they were growing up—a show of amusement, laced with sobriety. "Allow her to see that you are serious and well versed in those things that are most important. Keep your observations serious and grounded."

Serious and grounded. Conversation was not precisely Corbin's strength. Yet, the idea held the added bonus of not requiring he completely make himself over. He would simply talk to her on topics of appropriate seriousness. Certainly, he could manage that much.

* * *

Clara sat somewhat distanced from the children, watching them take their tea, which proved nothing more lavish than a platter of finger sandwiches and a glass of milk for each of them. A nursemaid assisted Alice with her meal, leaving Clara nothing to do besides watch and think.

Though she had originally left the sitting room fully intending to flee the house altogether, Clara found she hadn't the heart to pull the children away. They both seemed to be enjoying their new friend. So she had settled herself in an unobtrusive corner of the nursery to wait.

Why had the dowager seemed emotional? Clara didn't think she'd done anything to offend the lady. For the briefest of moments, she thought, perhaps, Corbin had said something unflattering to his mother about her. She dismissed the thought almost the moment she had it though. Corbin seemed too much a gentleman to act so shabbily.

As if her thoughts summoned him, Corbin walked into the schoolroom in the very next moment. Clara sat up straighter, determined to appear dignified, even in a schoolroom.

Alice waved at him. He nodded in acknowledgment and took a seat very near Clara.

"Good afternoon."

It seemed an odd thing to say. They had been in each other's company not twenty minutes earlier. He spoke as though they were meeting for the first time that day. "And to you," she returned through her confusion.

He sat silently a moment, brow furrowed as if in deep contemplation. "Things seem to be . . . Matters on the Continent are in quite a muddle. With Napoleon and . . . Wellington." He pushed out a breath that sounded somewhere between relieved and tense.

"Indeed," Clara replied. "Warfare is a difficult thing." *And an odd topic of conversation in a nursery.*

Corbin nodded ponderously. His look of concentration remained. The air of strain that hovered about him made her decidedly uncomfortable. She had, in recent days, found herself surprisingly relaxed in his company. He didn't worry her as much as he once had. But seeing him so tense made her decidedly ill at ease once more.

"The sermon was well delivered on Sunday."

How had that change of topic come about? Clara could not account for it. Still, she followed the tangent. "We are fortunate in our vicar."

"Indeed." His eyes darted about as if searching for something, though Clara couldn't say what. He abruptly spoke again, his words coming faster than before. "One must wonder if the uprising in the north cities—in the northern cities will recur. I believe Parliament is concerned the, ur, Luddites are not quite finished."

"I suppose only time will tell," Clara answered.

Tension pulled at Corbin's jaw. If he disliked the odd discussion so much, why did he continue it? For a time, it seemed he did not intend to.

They sat side by side in utter silence. Clara's eyes drifted to the children, though she surreptitiously watched Corbin as well. His brows remained furrowed even as his mouth moved silently. What had come over him? He'd never been talkative, yet he seemed strangely intent on discussing something, *anything*, with her. He'd veered from warfare to sermons to the Luddites with hardly a word of transition. As the minutes passed, he seemed to only grow more tense.

"There is a great deal going on. With . . . with the war."

"Yes, you mentioned the war already." How strange he was acting.

His eyes shifted to hers, a look of something very much like panic lingering there. What had brought that on? "Well . . ." His mouth moved silently again. "It is . . . It is important. And should be talked about. A sober-minded gentleman—or lady, certainly—she or he would want to discuss it. Not that I think you don't want to. Or maybe you don't."

He looked very nearly angry. What had happened? Was he angry with her? Frustrated at being forced into conversation? She certainly hadn't insisted on it.

"I like discussing those kinds of things. Important things." He wore a somber expression that did not seem to fit him, though he had never seemed frivolous.

"Apparently," Clara replied.

He grew noticeably uncomfortable and rose abruptly. "I . . . I have some things to see to."

Clara nodded, as confused as ever.

"Mister!"

They both looked at Alice. She grinned as she took a finger sandwich in each hand and proceeded to press them on either side of her face. Edmund sputtered into his milk. Alice giggled as bits of sandwich fell from her cheeks.

Clara bit her lips together, holding back laughter. It was precisely the sort of ill-mannered behavior she had feared but in the moment did not bring the horrified backlash she had anticipated. Caroline, far from being offended, grinned as she watched Alice repeat her actions.

"See, Mister?" Alice sounded quite pleased with herself. "Funny!" She pressed what little remained of her ill-used sandwiches to her face again, earning full laughs from her table companions and the nursemaid.

Corbin smiled at her as well. He shook his head in obvious amusement. Then his eyes met Clara's, and the laughter in them faded. He once again assumed the somber expression he'd worn earlier.

"Mister." Alice tugged on the leg of his pantaloons.

Clara bit back her warning that she be careful not to smear the mess from her hands all over him. The words would have come too late as it was. She shifted to the edge of her seat, ready to intervene should Corbin be upset over his ruined clothing.

"Yes, Alice?" He did not sound overly upset. He did not sound upset at all, in fact.

"I'm funny?" She offered him a sparkling smile.

"Yes," Corbin said. "You are being very funny today." Why, then, did he not sound entertained?

Alice patted her cheeks with her hands, this time free of her sandwiches. She dissolved into a fit of giggles. Clara allowed herself to smile. Corbin seemed undecided. The other two children laughed along with Alice.

"Finish your tea, sweetheart," Corbin quietly instructed.

Alice climbed back up on her little chair, looking quite pleased with her impromptu role as jester.

Corbin glanced back at Clara, uncertainty mixed with sobriety in his face. If not for the slightest hint of vulnerability she saw there, Clara might have been entirely put out with him. As it was, she watched him, trying to sort through the puzzle he presented.

Was he annoyed with them? Wishing the lot of them to Jericho? He had always been patient with the children and, though perhaps a little disapproving of her relatively humble circumstances, had never been unkind. They'd even exchanged a few amused observations earlier that day.

Why, then, had he been so unpersonable since arriving in the nursery? He could not possibly have been less enthusiastic about speaking with her.

"I need to go see to something." Corbin bowed a little awkwardly and swiftly left the room.

What a confusing man he is.

Chapter Twelve

"Here I come, Alice!"

Corbin recognized Edmund's voice. He had been riding Elf, trying to add a little natural dishevelment to the look he was attempting to affect. Appearing rough and carelessly powerful had proven harder than he'd anticipated.

After the abysmal failure of Harold's advice, he'd opted to try Jason's suggestion instead. He ought to have known any plan involving actually speaking was bound to be a bad idea. Clara had looked at him as though he were entirely out of his mind during his ill-fated trip to the nursery. And no wonder. He'd acted like an idiot, unable to stick to any topic, running out of things to say almost instantly.

Maybe Jason's advice would work better than Harold's had.

He dismounted, wrapping Elf's reins around an obliging branch, and inched forward, peeking through the trees. He'd nearly reached the small clearing that housed Ivy Cottage. Corbin wandered in that direction often.

"Where are you hiding, Alice?" Edmund called out, still amused and lighthearted.

The children were playing hide-and-seek, Corbin realized. He looked around the clearing and spotted Edmund.

"I am going to find you!" the boy called out, laughing as he knelt to look behind a small bush growing near the cottage.

Alice had, apparently, eluded Edmund. Corbin smiled at that. She was a precocious little thing.

Corbin searched the small clearing once more. Clara was nowhere in sight. He felt torn between disappointment and relief. He didn't feel entirely ready to display his well-rehearsed but still uncomfortable persona.

Corbin tugged a little at the collar of the shirt he wore. Hub from the stables was the closest in size to Corbin, but his clothing was not made of the most comfortable fabrics. And, Corbin had realized, the stable hand's neck was smaller than his. He'd had to leave the collar unbuttoned, something he would not usually consider doing.

The boots he wore still smelled strongly of the stable. They were his mucking boots, very nearly destroyed after years of working in them.

Corbin adjusted the shapeless hat on his head. It was yet another way he and Hub were not of a size. The blasted thing kept slipping half over his eyes.

He was beginning to doubt this latest attempt to capture Clara's attention. He probably looked more like a fool than the powerful, in-charge gentleman Jason had insisted he needed to portray.

"Alice?" Edmund's tone had intensified a little, which caught Corbin's attention. "Alice?"

Edmund looked a little frantic. Corbin quickly realized the game had come to an abrupt halt. Either Alice had really outdone herself hiding, or she was missing.

There weren't many places to hide in the small clearing or around the outside of the house. Edmund surely ought to have seen her by now. A thought occurred to Corbin that made his stomach clench. Suppose Alice had wandered into the thicket of trees? She would be very difficult to find.

"Alice?" Corbin called, quietly but urgently, looking all around him, his heart pounding. "Alice?"

Elf nickered, drawing Corbin's gaze. He tipped his head back enough to see from under the sagging brim of his borrowed hat. There, standing among the horse's powerful hooves was Alice, gazing up in wonder at Elf's underbelly.

Merciful heavens! His heart thudded to a halt. If something were to spook Elf, Alice could be trampled. "Alice," he whispered as gently as possible.

She turned her face toward him, one finger hooked over her lip.

Corbin inched forward, slipping off his hat so his view would not be impeded.

Recognition lit her beloved features. "Mister!" she called out.

Elf shifted slightly.

"Alice, dear." Corbin continued to talk softly, gesturing for her to keep quiet. "Don't move. Wait right there."

She scrunched her eyes a bit, focusing on him. Corbin smiled. She held her arms out as if asking to be held, one hand coming within inches of brushing Elf's right foreleg. That would have startled the horse for sure.

"Do you want to be held, dear?" Corbin asked, one eye on Elf, one eye on Alice.

She nodded and smiled even brighter.

"Very well." Corbin moved a little faster. "Let me come to you."

He was at Elf's head, then. Corbin gave him a reassuring rub on his nose, grateful Elf seemed calm. He patted the horse's shoulder, then squatted enough to reach out for Alice. The girl wrapped her arms around Corbin's neck, and he stood up.

Lud, she might have been trampled to death right in front of him.

"Oh, sweet Alice," he whispered, clutching her to him, holding her as tightly as he dared.

"Mister. You dirty."

He was, indeed. Dirty. Disheveled. A small pebble in his boot helped with the swagger. He pulled his hat on his head once more. Alice giggled. His new persona wasn't supposed to be funny.

"Shall I take you home?" Corbin asked Alice, knowing he needed to but beginning to seriously question the intelligence of his reinvention.

She shook her head no rather vehemently. Corbin watched her, puzzled. Alice pulled the brim of Corbin's hat over his eyes, then pulled it up again. Her eyes widened, her grin enormous. She repeated the gesture, acting surprised each time she lifted the brim and met his eyes.

"Edmund is worried about you, sweetheart," Corbin said quietly and continued walking toward the clearing, cursing the pebble that rubbed at the arch of his left foot, though knowing its presence was entirely his own doing.

Alice obviously knew where he was headed. She began to squirm and fuss. "No, Mister! I is hiding."

Afraid she'd slip into the forest again, Corbin held her tighter.

"Alice!" Edmund's voice cracked through the air.

Corbin caught sight of him running toward them. His infernal hat brim slid over his eyes again. He tried to push it back without letting go of Alice.

This wasn't happening right. His swagger had turned to a limp. He could hardly see around his hat. He knew he was filthy.

Alice fought tooth and nail to be let down, but Corbin knew she'd run back into the trees and probably right back to Elf. "No, Alice," he quietly implored. "You cannot hide in the trees."

She pointed to Edmund as he hurried toward them. She twisted harder, pulling at Corbin's hands.

"Put her down!" Edmund shouted. Corbin could hear him, but couldn't spot him. Infernal hat!

Something was hitting him. *Someone*, he guessed. Someone with small fists. Edmund? Then Alice started hitting him too, squealing so loudly Corbin couldn't make out Edmund's frantic words.

Corbin tipped his head from one side to the other, trying to get a look at his attackers. From the corner of his eye, he saw Clara.

That is a very large frying pan, was the last lucid thought he had before everything around him went black.

* * *

"Did you kill him?" Edmund asked.

Clara fervently hoped she had. She reached for the children, determined to pull them away. If Mr. Bentford had sent a ruffian after them, they had to run before he awoke. They had to get as far from him as possible.

"Mister!" Alice cried out, throwing herself on top of the inert man.

"Alice," Clara corrected, "this is not—" But she stopped and looked more closely. His hat had fallen back from his face. "Merciful heavens." She dropped to her knees on the ground beside him. It *was* Corbin. She hadn't even recognized him, hadn't been able to see his face. He was smudged with dirt, his hair disheveled, his clothing rough and worn. He'd been walking strangely.

"Mr. Jonquil?" Edmund asked in obvious alarm, sudden emotion in his voice. "He's dead!" Edmund wailed, tears surging down his face.

"He is not dead," Clara answered authoritatively. He wasn't dead, was he?

"You broke his face." Edmund continued his sobbing.

Corbin was already swelling. *Good heavens, I broke his face.* She reached out and gently touched the spreading redness. He winced, and Clara breathed a sigh of relief. He wasn't dead. Probably not even unconscious. He had likely only had the air knocked out of him.

"Broke face," Alice said sadly, scooting up Corbin's chest and touching his face with her tiny fingers. She leaned over and gingerly kissed his swelling cheek. Alice looked up at Clara and offered a proud smile.

"Yes, Alice, that will make the hurt better." She recognized Alice's imitation of her own cure for all ailments.

"Mama kiss," Alice instructed.

"No, Alice."

"You broke his face." Alice's tone felt like an accusation.

Edmund was looking at her in precisely the same way. Why shouldn't he? She'd single-handedly knocked Edmund's hero out cold.

Clara glanced warily down at Corbin, who still hadn't opened his eyes, though he appeared to be stirring. She wondered why he hadn't shaved or bathed or dressed with his usual care. What was the man thinking, showing up looking as he did? Of course she hadn't recognized him.

"Mama. Kiss."

"No."

"Mama." Alice's demand gained an edge of emotion.

Edmund looked near to tears once more.

Clara glanced warily at Corbin. A quick peck and the children would be satisfied. Her heart began pounding the instant she leaned over Corbin. She hated the very idea of such a thing.

Her breath stuck in her lungs. She wanted to simply stand up and run. Clara took a breath less than an inch from Corbin's face. He was dirty, but he smelled wonderful. Somehow, the smell of him eased her nerves a little. She was absolutely certain she would remember the smell of him for the rest of her life.

Slowly, her mind and heart loudly protesting, Clara lowered her face the last inch and lightly pressed a kiss on Corbin's face.

Hundreds of memories, each more unpleasant than the last, rushed through her as they always did when she came that close to a man. Clara pulled back but not much more than an inch as she attempted to prevent the tear in the corner of her eye from falling. How could she possibly explain that to the children? She would rather they not have further worries over their past.

She took another breath, a noseful of the smell of Corbin. Why did his scent calm her thudding heart? It still raced, but she wasn't nearly as close to panicking. It made no sense.

Clara looked down at the man in utter bewilderment and realized with a sudden resurgence of apprehension that his eyes were open, and he was watching her.

In a flash, she was on her feet, her breathing frantic. She tried to form words, tried to explain the predicament. Only four words came out. "I broke your face."

He nodded, looking at her wide-eyed. He was shocked at her behavior, at her forwardness. If he disapproved before, he would certainly do so now.

Had she, by kissing him, however innocently, given him the impression that she was free with her attentions?

Clara pulled herself up as regally and confidently as she could manage.

"Mister!" Alice squealed delightedly and clambered up his chest, wrapping her arms around his neck.

Corbin put one arm around Alice and managed to raise himself to a seated position with his other arm. He winced as Alice patted his cheek.

"Mister dirty." Alice smiled up at Corbin.

"Quite dirty." Clara hoped her voice sounded steady. "So much so, I didn't recognize you. I would not, I assure you, have hit you otherwise."

"If I had thought someone was abducting the children, I'd have knocked him flat as well," was the extent of Corbin's response.

"Then you aren't angry?" She hardly believed it possible.

Corbin just shook his head. Alice kissed his reddening face. He smiled at the girl.

Edmund, Clara suddenly realized, was sniffling. She turned her head to look at the boy, who was manfully attempting to hold back his tears.

Corbin ruffled Edmund's hair.

"I thought Aunt Clara killed you." Edmund's voice cracked with emotion.

"Not yet, Edmund," Corbin answered. "Not yet."

Not yet? What did he mean by that?

Corbin gingerly touched his own cheek. Clearly, even the gentle pressure was uncomfortable. She *had* hit him hard, as hard as she could, in fact.

"Come inside," she said. "I have an ointment that should take some of the sting out."

He looked uncertain.

"I promise not to hit you again." She allowed a fleeting smile.

That seemed to make his mind up. "Thank you," he said.

Keeping Alice in his arm, Corbin got to his feet. Edmund stepped up next to him, leaning against his side. Corbin set his free arm around Edmund's shoulders. Seeing her children in the grip of a stranger had terrified her to no end. But seeing them held so tenderly by Corbin finally brought her heart rate back to a calm pace.

They walked back into the house, the children not leaving Corbin's side. Clara motioned for him to take a seat, then slipped into the kitchen. She pulled a small jar of ointment from a drawer and returned with it to the sitting room.

Corbin sat on the sofa, the children on either side of him. Clara crossed to where Alice sat, picking her up and sitting in her place. Alice didn't accept her removal but sat on Corbin's lap instead. Clara met his gaze, silently asking if he wanted Alice to move. But he simply ran a hand down one of Alice's braids, not seeming the least put out at having her there.

Clara pulled the lid off the jar of ointment. "It doesn't have the most pleasant scent," she warned him. "But it does take the sting out."

"You know this from . . . from experience?" he asked.

She couldn't answer beyond a nod. An apothecary in Sussex had given her the recipe to treat the many injuries she'd sustained at Mr. Bentford's hands. The ointment worked wonders.

No words passed between them. Clara carefully dabbed ointment on the side of his face, offering an apologetic glance when he flinched at her touch. She had caused him pain, but he hadn't lashed out in return. He kept the children near, not rejecting them but offering the silent reassurance they needed.

Corbin Jonquil was proving himself different from the man she'd originally thought him to be, and she liked him more than she'd ever expected to. It was an unfamiliar and uncertain feeling.

Chapter Thirteen

"What happened ta yer face?"

Corbin grimaced. Until Jim asked that question, Corbin had held out some hope that the beginnings of a bruise on the side of his face might go unnoticed. He hadn't returned to the house, knowing Mater would notice instantly. He hadn't yet decided how to explain it, and he knew Mater would insist on an explanation.

"If ye were married, I'd think yer wife landed ye a facer." Jim laughed. "Ol' Bob's woman takes at him with her soup pot when he comes home swayin' drunk. Looks about like ye do, come the next morning."

"Bob shouldn't drink so much," Corbin answered, checking Whipster's hind hoof.

"Says the rum makes the soup pot easier to take," Jim replied.

Corbin set the hoof down and looked up at Jim, who smiled mischievously. *He drinks in order to tolerate his punishment for drinking?*

"It's enough to make a man never marry. No desire to take up drinkin' just to tolerate a wife."

Corbin smiled at that. Jim, who was all of sixty if he was a day, smelled perpetually of stable muck, had an equal number of teeth and limbs, and bore rather too close a resemblance to a pug. He wasn't likely to marry regardless of his feelings on drink and soup pots.

Devil's Advocate was running around the paddock again. The sight made Corbin think of Edmund. *I thought Aunt Clara killed you*, the boy had cried. Alice had seemed convinced of Corbin's demise as well. But it was the fear he'd seen in Clara's eyes that stuck with him. It hadn't seemed like fear for Corbin's wellbeing but fear of him.

Why would she be afraid of him? She'd kissed him, even if only a brief peck on the cheek. It was his first kiss, the first from a woman who was neither related to him nor under the age of six. That, he supposed, was what came of spending most of one's life in the stables.

But when their eyes had met in the moments after she'd kissed him, Clara's fear had retreated. She'd smiled. She'd invited him inside. How he'd managed to get through her ministrations without giving away his feelings, he didn't know. Having her so close, actually touching him, had made every thought, every breath more difficult than the last. All the while, he'd kept hoping she would kiss him again.

"So what did happen to yer phiz?"

"A frying pan." He didn't spare Jim so much as a glance. The man had interrupted a rather pleasant memory.

Jim laughed rather uproariously, making Devil's Advocate jump nervously at the sudden sound. "Known ye most of yer twenty-five years." Jim still laughed. "Ain't never known ye ta joke like that."

Corbin felt his face flush a little as he pushed away from the paddock fence.

"Gaw'law!" Jim's laughter died on the spot. "Ye ain't jokin'!"

His face, Corbin knew, reddened further.

"How'd ye come about having a fryin' pan knocked upside yer mug?"

Corbin simply didn't answer, knowing Jim would quickly realize and just as quickly accept that Corbin would not offer an explanation.

A shout echoed from within the stables, pulling Corbin's gaze in that direction.

"Sounds like Bernie," Jim said, naming the newest of the stable hands. "He knows better than to talk like that while there're ladies visiting Havenworth."

Corbin stepped inside the long stable building, fully expecting to find young Bernie at work mucking like he was supposed to be. But the lad was hunkered down in front of a stall, facing Charlie, of all people, a few piles of face cards in front of them.

"There blasted well better be a good explanation for this, Bernie," Jim growled, stomping past Corbin to where the young men sat.

Charlie and Bernie looked up at Jim's approach.

"Just a bit of a lark, Jim," Bernie explained.

"Ye've no time for larks, boy. Ye're supposed to be mucking stalls. That's what Mr. Jonquil's payin' ye for."

Bernie's face heated with embarrassment, his gaze dropping to his boots as he rose. "Yes, Jim. My apologies."

"I don't want yer apologies," Jim said. "I want ye in that stall working. Ye'll not be given another warning."

Bernie nodded quickly and slipped into a nearby stall. Corbin watched Charlie scoop up a small stack of coins and the cards. He too rose to his feet and made directly for the stable door. Apparently, Charlie thought he'd be permitted to leave without comment.

"Gambling, Charlie?"

Charlie shrugged. "Penny stakes."

"How many pennies did . . . did Bernie lose?"

Charlie's eyes reached Corbin's face. "What happened to your—"

"How much did he lose?" Corbin wouldn't allow a change of topic.

"Hardly anything."

Charlie tried to push past him, but Corbin blocked his exit.

"Not quite a pound," Charlie grumbled. "Nothing big."

A pound? Corbin shook his head in frustration. "That's a month's pay for him. A *month*."

To his credit, Charlie looked surprised. At least he hadn't knowingly fleeced the young stable hand. But he shouldn't have been gambling with the stable staff in the first place. "What were you thinking?"

"Fine." Charlie spun around, his posture one of obvious annoyance. "I'll give it back to him."

"No." Corbin shook his head. "This'll be a good . . . an important lesson for him."

Charlie's eyes looked everywhere but at Corbin. He probably realized he was in the wrong but wasn't entirely willing to admit it.

"No more gambling, Charlie."

Charlie gave a quick nod, then slipped out of the stables, heading toward the house. It was little wonder Mater was at her wit's end with her youngest. In the short time Charlie had been in residence at Havenworth, he'd managed to singe his bedchamber curtains, trample the newly budding tulips in the back garden, and break a window. Now he was bankrupting Corbin's staff.

When Corbin had assured Philip that he would look after the family, he hadn't entirely bargained on Charlie's troublemaking. Corbin had enough troubles of his own.

He lightly fingered his purpling face. It was more than a little sore. He'd never have guessed Mrs. Bentford could deliver such a felling blow. He felt a little better knowing she could. A woman living alone was vulnerable. That worried him about her. Often.

He looked around the stables. Without Edmund there, he had little to do. The stable staff was well organized and on task now that Charlie wasn't about. He really ought to go see to the rest of his visiting relatives, which, of course, meant explaining his face.

Corbin set his shoulders and made his way to the house. He took his time changing into his own clothes and washing his face and hands. A full bath would have to wait. He couldn't postpone the inevitable any longer. He entered the sitting room.

"Good heavens, Corbin," Mater exclaimed. "What have you done to your face?"

"Aunt Clara broke it."

Corbin spun on the spot and saw Edmund sitting on the floor, reading a picture book beside Caroline. What was Edmund doing there?

"She broke Corbo's face?" Caroline asked, perplexed.

"We thought he was a stranger," Edmund said.

"A stranger?" Mater asked, looking confused.

Corbin shot a glance at Jason, seated at the writing desk in the corner. Jason seemed oblivious to his own guilt in the debacle.

"Was your Aunt Clara very upset?" Mater sounded remarkably concerned by the possibility.

Clara had appeared extremely upset, in fact. Though she had administered to his injuries afterward.

"She said if Mr. Jonquil says I can't come to the stables anymore that I would have to come home," Edmund said, suddenly nervous and anxious looking. "And"—he locked eyes with Corbin—"I'm supposed to tell you that she's sorry she hit you."

"You didn't come to the stables," Corbin said quietly.

"Caroline wouldn't let me." Edmund gave Caroline an annoyed look.

Corbin looked to his niece, hoping for a more detailed explanation.

"Edmund is going to marry me." Caroline spoke as if it were an established fact. "So he has to like me better than horses."

"Why would I like a stupid old girl better than horses?" Edmund shot back.

That brought a quiver to Caroline's chin and instant moisture to her enormous blue eyes. She snapped closed the picture book, dropped it on the floor, and ran across the room into Charlie's arms. Charlie seemed as surprised by her choice of comforter as Edmund appeared to be by Caroline's sudden tears.

"Edmund." Corbin called to him quietly but sternly and motioned Edmund over to him. The boy moved slowly and far too warily. He obviously expected a severe scold.

"Yes, sir," Edmund muttered, head hung.

Corbin squatted in front of the boy, placing himself at Edmund's eye level. He laid a hand on the boy's shoulders. Edmund was trembling and tense. Snippets of conversations he'd had with him about the late Mr. Bentford rushed through Corbin's mind. Did Edmund think he meant to strike him?

"I know you prefer horses to girls." He spoke quietly, keeping the conversation private. "But you must not say so in a hurtful way, not to Caroline nor any other girl. And it is never permissible to tell a girl that she is stupid. Is that clear?"

"Yes, sir."

"And, Edmund?"

"Yes, sir?"

Corbin chucked the boy on the chin, drawing his eyes upward. Corbin smiled. "I used to think horses were better than girls as well."

"Do you still?" Some of Edmund's tension eased.

Corbin silently shook his head. No, he certainly did not think so any longer.

Edmund made a face, communicating obvious disagreement.

"Apologize to Caroline," Corbin gently prodded.

Edmund trudged across the room. "I'm sorry I was mean," Edmund muttered.

Caroline pouted and continued to cling to Charlie.

"Good apology," Charlie evaluated aloud.

"Excellent apology," Jason agreed from across the room.

"Caroline." Corbin allowed the tiniest hint of a reprimand to enter his tone.

She looked momentarily shocked. Mater did as well, though Corbin managed to ignore it. If Edmund was to learn to treat girls and ladies kindly, he would have to see some fruit from his efforts.

"I forgive you," Caroline said.

"Can we read the book now?" Edmund asked impatiently.

"You don't want to play with the horses?" Caroline's pout remained firmly in place.

Edmund shrugged. "It's a good book so far."

Caroline's face split into an all-encompassing grin. "I knew you'd like it!" She climbed off Charlie's lap and hurried back across the room to their abandoned storybook.

"Layton might not appreciate knowing Caroline is doggedly pursuing a young man already," Jason said, having moved closer without Corbin realizing it. "Have you put a cold cloth on that bruise? It looks awful."

Corbin shot Jason a look that sent him instantly stepping backward.

"What?" Jason's eyes widened.

There was no opportunity to answer. Simmons entered in that moment and announced a visitor.

"Miss Mariposa Thornton."

Jason's head snapped in the direction of the door. "What the bl—"

Corbin elbowed him in the ribs in time to cut off the curse. If Harold had been present, they would have been subjected to an entire sermon on the evils of coarse language.

A young lady, probably little more than five feet tall, all black curls and almond-shaped dark eyes, stepped into the room, quickly surveying the entire assembly. Her gaze fell on Jason, and her eyebrows raised triumphantly.

"Well." She smiled smugly, speaking with an obvious Spanish accent. "*Ahí estás*, Mr. Jonquil. You, *señor*, are a difficult man to locate."

"What the bl—"

"Language, *señor*!" Miss Thornton interrupted, her shock too theatrical to be sincere.

"You were instructed to direct all correspondence to my secretary," Jason said in clipped tones.

Miss Thornton raised a sleek black eyebrow. She walked past Jason, quite unconcerned that she was being skewered with a look that had brought more than one witness to the breaking point in a court room. Corbin knew that look—he'd seen Jason at work before.

"If I wanted a correspondent," she said, her gestures every bit as expressive as her face and a perfect match for her accent, "I would write to my *abuela*."

"Your *abuela* lives with you." Jason sounded increasingly disgruntled.

"So you can see how pointless letter writing can be." Miss Thornton spoke as if Jason had just agreed wholeheartedly with her. "And you must be Mater." The young lady addressed Mater with no hint of embarrassment or intimidation.

"How did you . . . ?"

"Your son speaks of you often."

"Jason?"

Miss Thornton laughed, waving her hand in a dismissive gesture. "Not that one. The *capitán*."

"You know Stanley?" Mater was on her feet, clasping the young lady's hands. Until that moment, Corbin hadn't realized how worried Mater truly was over Stanley's safety.

"*Sí*." Miss Thornton smiled at her. "When the fighting was in España. Our *casa* was used by the British. I knew him then. And again at Ortez. He is a good man. Not useless like that one." She waved her hand toward Jason.

Corbin looked in that direction. He'd never seen Jason so close to losing his composure.

So much for being in control of every situation, Corbin thought.

"Corbin, may we use your library?" Jason asked through clenched teeth. "I believe Miss Thornton has some business to discuss."

Corbin nodded.

"You are Señor Corbin?" Miss Thornton hurried across the room without managing to look as though she were hurrying. "As you see, I have met your evil twin."

There was an ocean of mischief in Miss Thornton's eyes, and Corbin found himself smiling down at her, liking her on the spot.

"Come, Miss Thornton," Jason instructed tensely.

"It was wonderful to meet all of you," Miss Thornton offered to the room in general.

"Now," Jason snapped.

Miss Thornton shook her head daintily, then made her way from the room as slowly as humanly possible.

The moment the door closed, Charlie burst out laughing. "She is perfect," he declared between gasps.

"Miss Thornton is near to driving poor Jason out of his mind." A smile tugged at Mater's lips as she made the observation.

Good, Corbin thought, remembering the horrid advice Jason had given him regarding women. *Very good.*

* * *

Clara couldn't sit and wait any longer. Edmund hadn't returned immediately from Havenworth. That had to be a good sign. But Suzie said he'd gone inside the house at the invitation of young Caroline Jonquil and her nurse. Clara had no idea what reception, if any, he'd received from Corbin.

Edmund loved the time he spent in the stables. If he lost that because of her, Clara would never forgive herself. Corbin had let her apply the ointment, and he hadn't yelled or scolded. But she couldn't be certain he hadn't harbored a grudge.

There was nothing for it but to go see him. Suzie agreed to look after Alice while Clara was gone. Clara tied the ribbon of her bonnet firmly under her chin and strode determinedly toward Havenworth.

She would simply reason with him, explain that accosting him had been entirely her fault and he ought not to punish Edmund for it. Self-implicating pleadings had worked wonders with Mr. Bentford. He had been rather easily convinced of her guilt in all things. Taking the blame upon herself for every little thing had made life easier for Edmund.

Over and over, Clara rehearsed her speech. She hardly noticed the passing scenery, nor how quickly she approached Havenworth. She'd cut through the small copse of trees separating their properties, that being the shortest route.

"Surely you must know how pleased I am to see you." A voice sounded from among the trees. "There's no need to pretend you aren't pleased to see me as well."

Instantly, Clara was alert and on her guard. She knew Mr. Finley's voice the way a person recognized the sound of an angry dog—it instantly announced danger. She realized in the next moment that Mr. Finley was not talking to her.

"You never seemed to be at any of the functions I attended in Town," Mr. Finley continued.

Clara moved quickly, quietly. She spotted him. He was close on the heels of a young lady, probably Clara's age, who seemed to be quite determinedly walking away from him. *Good for her*, Clara thought.

"If I didn't know better, Catherine, I would think you have been avoiding me." Mr. Finley reached out and took hold of the lady—Catherine, he'd called her—by the wrist. She managed to wrench free of him, walking even faster.

"Catherine." Mr. Finley chuckled. The laugh, however, was menacing, with an edge of frustration. Mr. Finley was growing tired of civilities. Clara shivered at the thought. What might he do if Catherine's rejections pricked too deeply at his pride?

"I have never given you leave to use my Christian name," Catherine snapped, not slowing as she spoke.

"Your husband is not here to object to the intimacy."

Clara saw the woman stiffen and recognized the stature for what it was: fear. She understood well the effect a man could have on an unprotected woman when his intent was blatantly dishonorable.

"Stop this ridiculous posturing, Catherine." Mr. Finley was nearly growling. "You are making a fool of yourself pretending to be offended by my attentions. I am not a patient man."

Searching frantically around her while still keeping pace with Mr. Finley and his prey, Clara finally spotted a large branch lying on the ground. She picked it up and quietly approached Mr. Finley from behind. He was too intent on discomposing his victim to notice her approach.

With a swing so hard she grunted at the effort, Clara whacked the branch across the back of Mr. Finley's knees, sending him toppling to the ground. She lifted the branch up high and brought it crashing down on his head.

Mr. Finley was probably no more than stunned. Not wanting to take any chances, she ran ahead to where the poor woman, pale and obviously stricken by the situation, stood staring.

"Come." Clara took hold of the lady's hand and pulled her along at a run, away from Mr. Finley, praying they reached Havenworth before Mr. Finley recovered his senses.

Chapter Fourteen

"I WILL EXPLAIN TO YOUR husband." Clara managed the words, even in her growing breathlessness as they rushed toward Havenworth. "I will tell him it was my fault." She wasn't certain how to convince him of that, but she would manage it somehow.

The lady running with her appeared to be fighting tears.

"He won't blame you," Clara assured her. "I'll think of something to tell him so he won't be angry with you."

She didn't slow their pace until they reached the steps of Havenworth. The butler let them in after a swift glance at the face of Clara's companion. He went so far as to hurry quite unbutlerlike up the stairs, motioning for them to follow.

Clara recognized the room before they stepped inside: Corbin's library.

The Havenworth butler didn't even stop to announce them. The woman Clara knew only as Catherine rushed inside and directly into the arms of a man whose dark hair and dark eyes set him apart from the Jonquils. Clara stayed near the door. Though Catherine seemed to trust this man, Clara didn't know him from Adam.

"What in heaven's name?" the man muttered as Catherine began sobbing in his embrace.

"Mr. Finley," Catherine managed to say.

Clara saw tension instantly clench the man's jaw. "Catherine." The gentleman pulled the still-crying woman a little away from him and looked into her face.

Clara opened her mouth to explain. The poor lady did not deserve her husband's wrath after what she'd just endured.

"Did he hurt you?" Catherine's husband asked. "Did he hurt you in any way? Any way at all?"

Clara's words stopped unuttered. *Did he hurt you?* No lectures on propriety? On entering a room like a lady? No suspicious questioning of her whereabouts?

Catherine answered the man's questions with a shake of her head.

Clara stared, mesmerized, utterly confused.

"Are you certain?"

Catherine nodded.

The man turned to look at Clara. "Did he hurt *you*?" he asked.

Clara could only stare. This stranger was concerned for *her*? Was the lecture, the explosion of temper to come later, then?

"She ambushed him, Crispin," Catherine's shaky voice announced. "And then we ran."

"Blasted—" He muttered the rest of the curse under his breath.

"Crispin?" Corbin's voice came from the doorway just behind Clara. "Simmons said—" He stopped abruptly. Clara felt his gaze on her without looking back. "Mrs. Bentford." His shock was obvious.

Clara turned then, meaning to offer a polite curtsy. She froze, however, the moment she saw his bruised face. Good heavens, had she really hit him that hard? He was purple from temple to jaw on the left side of his face. Not even the ointment, which had done wonders for many of her own bruises over the years, had kept his face from discoloring so quickly.

"Finley's on your land, Corbin," Crispin said. "He accosted Catherine."

"Is she hurt?" Corbin's eyes instantly filled with concern.

Never had Clara encountered one gentleman, let alone two, who would concern himself so instantly with the welfare of a woman. She didn't understand it.

"She's fine. Thanks to Mrs. Bentford."

"I hit him," Clara explained, feeling the need to tell Corbin. "With a stick."

"Not a frying pan?" Corbin asked with dry amusement.

She nearly smiled. But the graveness of the situation settled over her once more. In an instant, she was shivering. "I think he meant her harm," Clara whispered, hearing the unexpected panic in her voice. "I think he truly intended to hurt her."

"I don't doubt he did." Corbin watched her rather too closely for comfort. "He is selfish and dishonorable. A . . . a bounder and a womanizer and—"

"I know." Clara clutched her hands together to keep them from shaking. She could easily have been the one in the forest, alone and accosted by Mr.

Finley. Despite having grown braver and stronger over the past months, she couldn't seem to stop her reaction to the danger she'd only narrowly escaped.

"But Finley was at your home."

"Uninvited," Clara said.

"He called you *my dear*." Corbin's gaze didn't waver.

"That is also what he called Catherine," Clara said. "I didn't like it any more than she seemed to."

Corbin's eyes narrowed, his expression growing questioning. Such scrutiny from a man usually made her antsy. Instead, she found herself growing warm and, most likely, flushed.

"If you will excuse us." Crispin stepped around Clara and Corbin toward the door. "I am going to ask Jason and Charlie to have a look around to make certain Finley has left."

Corbin's gaze shifted to Crispin. "Have the staff . . . the stable staff do the same."

Clara and Corbin were suddenly alone. He looked at her once again. Heavens, he had the bluest eyes. And the purplest face.

"I did that," Clara whispered, touching his face lightly. "I am sorry. I truly am."

Corbin didn't say anything. His breathing tensed. His eyes darted around the room.

Clara's mind screamed that she was in danger. Yet, she wasn't afraid. She let her hand drop back to her side. "Is Edmund here?"

Corbin nodded. "With Caroline."

There was a stiff and awkward pause. Clara stood on needle points, with no idea what Corbin would do next. She had never known anyone like him and could not possibly anticipate his actions.

"Did you . . . Were you wanting—?" He stopped abruptly, muttering something under his breath that Clara couldn't make out. "Do you want to take Edmund home?"

"I think that would be best." She felt inexplicably close to tears. Clara forced them back, muscled down the lump in her throat. Why in heaven's name was she so nearly crying?

"I will . . . I can have a carriage called up for you," Corbin said, then bowed and left the room.

Clara pressed her hand to her heart to still the painful thudding she felt there. Such a powerful reaction was strange, unexpected. Somehow, Corbin Jonquil had pierced her defenses. He affected her in odd and inexplicable ways.

Edmund's praise and Alice's obvious love had first endeared Corbin to Clara. She couldn't decide if her experience was the accurate foreteller or if she ought to trust her children's evaluation.

The only thing she felt certain of was that she needed time and room to sort things out.

* * *

"Finley's gone," Charlie announced to those in the sitting room after returning from the search conducted around the grounds of Havenworth. Jason nodded his confirmation.

Catherine sat on the sofa beside Crispin, her head resting on his shoulder, his arm holding her to him. Corbin wondered what that felt like, being able to comfort the woman he loved. Clara had certainly been upset by the encounter as well. She'd seemed on edge. What had he been able to do for her? Call a carriage.

It was frustrating.

"I never liked that George Finley," Mater said. "Your father warned Robert that his son was not turning out well. But Robert Finley continued to indulge George in absolutely everything. Now that spoiled boy has grown into a man who does not warrant the title of gentleman. He feels the world owes him anything he wants, and he takes it without regard to propriety."

"Perhaps I should take Catherine home," Crispin said.

Mater shook her head. "I am certain that is not necessary. Corbin's stable staff can help keep an eye out."

"And what about Mrs. Bentford?" Catherine asked quietly. "I don't imagine Mr. Finley will appreciate having been thwarted by a lady."

Corbin rubbed his face with his hand. He was not technically in a position to offer his assistance to Clara. But Catherine's words had a ring of truth. Finley had already shown an interest in Clara. That was not likely to subside because she had rescued Catherine. Quite the opposite, in fact. Finley would make besting her a matter of regaining his pride.

"Ivy Cottage can . . . We can, if—" He let out a frustrated breath. Why could he never seem to manage a whole, articulate sentence? Corbin organized his thoughts. *Someone from the stables can keep an eye on Ivy Cottage. Someone from the stables can keep an eye on Ivy Cottage.* "Someone from the stables can keep an eye on Ivy Cottage."

"Excellent suggestion." Jason nodded his approval, though he seemed distracted. Jason's mind had been elsewhere all afternoon.

"We could always wait until Layton arrives tomorrow, break into Finley Grange, and steal all of Finley's underclothes," Crispin said.

Corbin, Jason, and Crispin laughed at the memory from Eton. Charlie looked far too intrigued. Mater seemed to barely suppress a chuckle herself. Corbin wondered if she had heard about that infamous incident. Most likely. Mater had known most all of their escapades as youth, a fact that had surprised and intrigued them all.

"Only if you promise to fly every single pair from the windows of Westminster," Catherine said, earning further laughs and an amused kiss on the cheek from her husband.

Corbin felt a stab of jealousy at seeing that gesture. He turned away, thinking. Clara had kissed him. But, then, it had been little more than a peck. He wanted to find that encouraging, but it was so little to build on.

Catherine and Crispin hadn't had the easiest or smoothest of beginnings. Yet, one look at them together confirmed they were deeply in love with each other. What did Crispin do differently from him?

Corbin's eyes settled on Jason, slumped in a chair in the corner, forehead creased, something like a confused scowl on his face. It was the same look he'd worn since Miss Thornton's unforgettable visit earlier in the day.

"You're a Jonquil," Corbin's brother Layton had once told him. "Of course women will think you're an idiot."

Perhaps his brothers were not the best source to look to for guidance when wooing a lady. But his own efforts so far didn't appear to be working either.

It was too much to think about at the moment. Corbin reminded himself he really ought to head to the stables to set up a watch on Ivy Cottage.

He'd only just left the sitting room when Mater's voice called out to him. "Corbin?"

He turned and watched as she hurried to where he stood.

"May I walk with you?" she asked.

Corbin nodded, offering his arm, which she took. "I was . . . I was going to—"

"The stables?" She finished for him with a smile. "I could have guessed. The stables always were where you were headed."

That was certainly true.

They stepped out of the house and began the short trek to the stables, a soft breeze blowing.

"Have I ever told you I am proud of what you have done here?" Mater said, looking around her. "You were so young when you began. I worried for you. You did not have your father to advise you, and Philip, bless his heart, was quite young himself. But look at all you've done."

Corbin felt himself color at her praise. He'd never been comfortable with attention, even from his own mother.

"All of you boys have far exceeded my expectations," Mater continued. "Well, Charlie is still a work in progress."

Corbin laughed at that. He smiled at Mater when he realized she was watching him.

"It is good to hear you laugh, Corbin. You seldom used to laugh out loud." She seemed to study him, which made Corbin instantly nervous. "Something has changed with you, for the better. You talk a little more and with a little more confidence."

He didn't feel more confident. Less, in fact. Clara was too much of a mystery, too hard to understand. His inability to decipher her reactions to him, to find a way to make a positive impression on her was frustrating to no end. What did she see so lacking in him?

They had reached the stables, and catching sight of the man he was looking for, Corbin called out to him. Jim began walking toward him.

"Are you setting up your watch?" Mater asked.

Corbin nodded. "I don't like the idea of . . . Mrs. Bentford ought to have someone looking out for her."

Mater nodded. "I cannot help but find it telling that she successfully felled two grown men in a single day." Mater's eyes slid to Corbin's bruised face. "If I had to guess, I would say she has experience defending herself physically against men. Not a very comforting thought."

Comforting? Hardly. Corbin felt every muscle in his body tense at the truthful ring of Mater's conjecture. Someone had hurt Clara, he was certain of it. Could that, then, be part of the puzzle? She'd been hurt and, therefore, was wary. He couldn't say for certain.

He might not be able to make her care for him, but, he swore, he would make it his business to see that she was not hurt again.

Chapter Fifteen

Clara hadn't seen Corbin in four days. He'd sent a remarkably large groom to Ivy Cottage each afternoon to accompany Edmund to Havenworth. The same groom, or one nearly as large, always brought him back. In yet another way, Clara found herself indebted to Corbin Jonquil. He was not in the least obligated to look after her, yet he was doing precisely that.

She had come to church this morning unusually nervous. She'd tried to convince herself over the past few days she had no reason to be unsettled over him. Despite her efforts, she was entirely unsettled. She had come to trust him, at least a little, and until she could explain to herself why this was, her nervousness remained.

To her utter bewilderment, she wanted to see him again. She had, in an odd sort of way, missed him, despite the fact that they didn't meet all that often. Perhaps it was nothing more than wanting to see *which* Corbin Jonquil would arrive at services today. Would he be dressed flamboyantly or like a street sweeper? Would he talk aimlessly on and on or sit in silence? Would he be the confusing, unpredictable man he sometimes was or the gentle man who treated her little family with such tenderness?

The entire congregation hushed as the Jonquil party entered, just as they had the previous Sunday. Grompton was unaccustomed to the nobility sitting amongst them. Clara refused to look back and gawk at their entrance. The attention, she knew, made Corbin uncomfortable.

There was something of a commotion behind her. Clara determinedly faced forward.

"Mrs. Bentford?"

She didn't have to look to know it was Corbin. His voice had become as familiar to her as either of the children's. He stood at the edge of their pew.

"May I . . . I—"

A chuckle sounded behind her. Clara saw Corbin shoot a look at whomever sat there.

"There isn't . . . I don't—" He stopped abruptly, the way he often did. Now why did that make her want to smile? "There is no more room on the pew with my family."

Clara was not sure how that fact related to her or why Corbin had brought it to her attention.

"Might I . . . Would you be put out if . . . if I asked to join you?"

"Your family won't make room for you?" she asked, surprised.

Corbin looked frustrated as he shook his head.

Clara glanced over her shoulder. Charlie and Jason were directly behind her, both looking as though they were barely holding back their laughter. What was it, she wanted to know, that they found so funny? Did they expect to make her uneasy?

She refused to be humiliated. Her days of enduring embarrassment and torment were gone now.

"Of course you may sit with us." She slid Edmund, Alice, and herself down the pew to the far end, allowing Mr. Jonquil plenty of room.

"Mister!" Half the congregation must have heard Alice's whispered exclamation.

Corbin sat closer to them than she had anticipated. Alice climbed onto his lap, and he looked at Clara, causing her heart to beat frantically in her throat.

"Thank you for letting me. . . for allowing me to—" He stopped short.

Clara nodded her understanding of what he'd at least partially said. She took a deep breath. She was sitting directly beside him; only Edmund separated them. She ought to have felt nervous, uneasy. Instead, she was unexpectedly content at having him nearby.

Throughout the seemingly interminable services, Alice played with Corbin's cravat and the buttons on his waistcoat. Edmund continually gazed at his idol, admiration unmistakably written on his face.

When Corbin began stroking Alice's hair as she sat on his lap, head pressed to his chest, Clara found herself watching his hands, mesmerized. They were large, strong hands. Yet at that moment, they were engaged in an act of extreme gentleness. It was a paradox. So much about him was.

What would it feel like, she wondered, to be held in arms that were at once powerful and tender? Clara blushed immediately. *Pay attention to the sermon*, she scolded herself. *Quit building castles in the sky.*

She fully expected Corbin to hand Alice back to her when the sermon ended and leave with his family. But he simply rose, keeping Alice firmly in his arms, then paused, waiting for Clara and Edmund to stand as well. With a smile but not a word of explanation, he accompanied them to the back doors of the chapel and out into the courtyard, where the rest of the Jonquils and Lord and Lady Cavratt waited for him.

Clara spotted among the group a couple she hadn't seen before. Though built on a slightly larger scale, the gentleman was clearly a Jonquil. Beside him stood a lady, probably not quite Clara's age, with fiery red hair and an easy, natural smile.

"Mrs. Bentford," Corbin suddenly spoke, "may I introduce to you my brother, Mr. Layton Jonquil of Farland Meadows." The new arrival inclined his head. "And this is . . . is his wife, Lady Marion Jonquil."

Lady? Heavens, were they all titled?

"Layton and Marion, this is . . . this is Mrs. Bentford. Of Ivy Cottage. Her nephew is Edmund Clifton."

Layton—there was no escaping thinking of them by their Christian names with so many Mr. Jonquils about—nodded. His smile seemed to indicate that he had only recently taken up the habit of smiling with regularity. Clara felt herself tense.

"Is this the Edmund who is Caroline's intended?" Layton asked.

"Her *what*?" Clara sputtered.

"Caroline has declared that Edmund is going to marry her, will he or nill he." Layton's smile broadened. He looked at his wife. "There has been a great deal of marrying in the family lately."

Lady Marion colored a little, though she laughed. "Caroline has succumbed to the power of suggestion, I suppose."

"I hope the children at least plan to invite us." Clara forced the lighthearted reply but watched Layton warily. He was larger than all of the others.

"I hope your nephew plans to ask for my permission to pay his addresses," Layton added.

They all turned to look at Edmund, who was pointedly ignoring Caroline. She, however, was chattering on as if he were raptly attentive.

"Perhaps Caroline ought to be the one asking permission," Lady Marion said with a hint of laughter. "She seems to be the only one paying any addresses."

"Mater is ready to leave." Jason stepped into the conversation. Layton and Lady Marion took Caroline in hand and began making their way toward the waiting carriages. Jason followed.

Clara breathed a sigh of relief. She turned to Corbin. Alice's arms hung limp at her sides, her cheek flattened against Corbin.

"I think she is asleep," Clara said.

Corbin nodded. "She's been drooling down my collar ever since we left the chapel."

"Oh, I am sorry."

Corbin only shook his head.

"I will take her home and put her to bed." Clara held her arms out to receive the bundle.

"There is room in the carriage. You would . . . She would be home more quickly."

"I do not want to put you out." Clara offered him the means of escaping his gesture.

"It is not an imposition," he replied quietly.

"You're certain there is room?"

Corbin nodded toward the waiting line of Jonquil carriages. Clara looked as well. The rear carriage sat empty, the rest of the party having climbed into the other two.

She felt immediate relief at the idea of not walking home and the tiniest niggle of excitement at spending more time with Corbin.

"It would be nice not to walk the four miles with a sleep-heavy child," she admitted. "Alice has grown so much lately that I find my arms positively ache by the time we reach Ivy Cottage."

Corbin motioned Edmund toward the waiting carriage. He held Alice with one hand and helped Clara inside with the other. The simple feel of her hand in his did odd things to Clara's breathing. She did her best to ignore the sensation.

He allowed Alice to continue slumbering against his chest as the carriage rumbled toward Ivy Cottage. Edmund was sleepy as he often was on Sundays after services. The ride was a quiet one. Clara's eyes were drawn to Corbin as they had been throughout the sermon. The bruise on his face remained in evidence, though greatly improved.

"I am sorry about hitting you with the pan." Clara broke the silence but kept her voice low so as not to disturb the children. "I truly did not recognize you. With the hat and everything."

"I was looking rather unkempt." Corbin seemed embarrassed by the memory. She thought of him dressed in overly vibrant colors some weeks earlier and remembered he'd been embarrassed then too.

"We've bored Edmund to sleep," Clara said, realizing the boy had drifted off, his face pressed to the glass window of the carriage.

"He worked very hard at the stables yesterday," Corbin said.

She saw fondness in Corbin's eyes as he gazed at Edmund, and though she hadn't expected it, Clara liked seeing it.

"He will probably sleep for some time," Corbin added.

"Except he has grown too big for me to carry." Clara felt disappointed for the boy—Edmund would have appreciated the nap. "He'll have to awaken to go inside."

"I will carry him," Corbin offered without hesitation.

"But you have Alice."

He smiled across at her, and Clara's insides flip-flopped.

"I can carry them both," he said.

A few minutes later, he proved his claim. Clara led Corbin up the stairs, Alice in one arm, Edmund in the other. Alice hardly even shifted as Corbin gently laid Edmund on his bed. Edmund turned onto his side, as he always did, and curled into a tight ball. Clara laid his blanket on top of him.

"He truly was tired," Corbin said as they walked out the door of Edmund's room and through the door to Alice's.

"He is often irritable on the walk home from church. I think he is exhausted." Again, more personal comments she hadn't intended to utter.

Corbin slowly lowered Alice onto her bed, smoothing back her hair and watching her for a moment. "She's an angel," Corbin whispered.

"Yes, but only when she's sleeping." Clara laughed lightly.

Corbin smiled over at her. "I doubt that."

That smile tied her tongue. She knew she was blushing. What in heaven's name was happening to her?

"Thank you for bringing us home." Clara suddenly found herself anxious to be alone. "And helping with the children."

"Not at all," he answered quickly, awkwardly.

They stood in heavy silence for a moment, neither looking at the other, though Clara couldn't possibly have been more aware of his presence. She needed time to sort things out, to discover how this entirely confusing man had made her react so uncharacteristically to him.

"My family will be expecting me," Corbin said.

Clara managed to bite back a sigh of relief as she nodded her head in agreement.

"Good day, Mrs. Bentford."

"Good day," Clara answered.

Once his footsteps echoed back to silence, she dropped into a chair near Alice's bed and rubbed her throbbing temples. She, who had learned long ago never to trust any man, wasn't afraid of this one. And more than that, she had a nagging suspicion that she had come to care for him. He seemed kind and good. He seemed trustworthy. But was he?

How she wanted him to be.

* * *

"I am bored," Edmund moaned.

Clara bit back a sigh of frustration. It had been a difficult day. Corbin had apparently been quite busy showing various horses to prospective buyers and hadn't had as much time for Edmund as usual. So Edmund was sulking.

Alice was cutting teeth and, therefore, had been cross. By some miracle, Clara had coaxed the girl to sleep. Without Suzie to help—she was visiting a friend for a couple of days—the task of keeping both children content was wearing on Clara.

"Why don't you read the book Mr. Jonquil gave you?" Clara hoped Edmund would stop kicking his chair. The repetitive thumping was driving her mad.

"I already read it," Edmund grumbled.

"Perhaps—"

A knock at the door cut off her words. Clara's heart fluttered. Corbin had come to see her at last—she hadn't seen him in twenty-four hours. She rushed to the door and pulled it open.

But it wasn't Corbin.

"Squire Reynolds." She'd known him in Sussex but hadn't seen him since leaving there more than six months earlier.

"Good evening, Mrs. Bentford." The man doffed his hat.

"What brings you to Nottinghamshire?" She'd never known the squire to wander much more than the ten miles or so required for him to reach the assizes.

"You do, actually," he answered, shifting uncomfortably.

I do. The vague sense of alarm she'd always felt with each knock at the door returned with full force. He'd come from Sussex, from the very neighborhood, in fact, that she had fled. And he had come specifically for her. No one in that neighborhood was supposed to know where she was.

Squire Reynolds was the sort of easily persuaded man who did almost nothing on his own and whose convictions shifted with alarming regularity. And the person he was most often influenced by was the very person she was hiding from.

"Won't you come in?" Clara took a deep breath. Squire Reynolds, taken on his own, was not a threat. If she kept their interaction friendly, he might be sent on his way without incident.

He nodded and looked decidedly uneasy. Clara closed the door behind him and ushered him into the sitting room. Edmund came immediately to her side, clinging and anxious.

"You said *I* brought you to Nottinghamshire." Clara used the tone of authority she'd learned to affect to protect herself. "I would appreciate an explanation."

He twisted the brim of his hat in his hands and kept his eyes diverted. Clara felt her stomach twist as well. Something was wrong. Clara pushed back her growing sense of panic.

"I am sent to take you back to Sussex, Mrs. Bentford."

Sussex was the last place she ever wanted to go. For six months, she'd had her first taste of freedom. She would not go back.

"You are scheduled to stand trial at the assizes next month," the squire continued. "I am charged with returning you to Sussex to await the hearing."

Clara felt the blood drain from her face. She struggled to wrap her mind around what she was hearing. She'd fully expected Mr. Bentford to make some effort at dragging her back to Sussex. But she had never in her worst imaginings anticipated this. "What is the crime of which I stand accused?"

"Assault," Squire Reynolds answered. "You are accused of beating a man with a fire poker. And there is, I am afraid, sufficient evidence to support the charge."

"Oh heavens," Clara muttered, clutching the chair.

"You will have to return, Mrs. Bentford."

"This is ludicrous," Clara said, her voice strangled even to her own ears. "I haven't—"

"Enough protests, Clara," a voice said from the doorway, and she all but fainted. "You know perfectly well there is nothing ludicrous about this."

Edmund whimpered beside her.

"Run, Edmund," Clara whispered. "Run all the way to Havenworth. Do not stop until you find help."

He didn't need to be told twice.

As she'd anticipated, the new arrival ignored Edmund's flight and focused instead on her. She forced herself to meet his eyes. A shiver of sheer terror ran down her spine. He'd found her. Somehow, Mr. Bentford had found her.

Chapter Sixteen

"You're sure you won't part with Happy Helper?" Crispin asked.

Corbin shook his head. "Edmund would never forgive me."

"You've become rather attached to that boy," Layton said, joining the discussion.

Corbin couldn't deny it.

"And his aunt, I'd say," Jason added.

"Mrs. Bentford doesn't even think Corbin is useless," Crispin said. "Which is more than we can say for a certain lady's opinion of *you*."

Corbin laughed, as did Layton, who had been informed of Miss Thornton's visit in tremendous detail. Jason, however, didn't seem amused.

"Mr. Jonquil?"

They all turned at the greeting. Corbin, however, recognized Seth from the stables. He nodded for the boy to continue.

"Thought you'd wanna know someone's come to the Widow Bentford's cottage," Seth said. "'Tweren't Mr. Finley though. Ain't no one I've ever seen."

Odd.

"She let him in," Seth continued. "Must have known 'im. I came an' told you soon as I saw 'im go in."

Corbin nodded his gratitude, and Seth made his way to the stable.

"What do you want to do, Corbin?" Layton asked.

"It's probably nothing." But he didn't feel easy. He had a bad feeling, though he couldn't explain it.

"Wouldn't hurt to go check," Jason said.

Convinced he was overreacting but unable to sit still, Corbin nodded and began making his way to the trees that separated their properties.

Layton stopped him. "Might as well ride. It would be faster. Just in case."

There was some wisdom in that. Corbin hadn't, however, anticipated the others coming along.

"In case you need a chaperone," Layton explained with a smile. Crispin grinned as well. Those two could be as bad as Philip sometimes.

They'd barely reached the trees when Corbin spotted Edmund running as if the hounds of hell were chasing him. Corbin reined Elf in.

"Edmund!" he called out to him.

The boy immediately shifted direction, heading directly for him. With rising concern, Corbin realized Edmund was crying.

"What's happened?" Corbin quickly dismounted and held his arms open to the boy. Edmund threw himself into Corbin's arms.

"He came." Edmund's sobs grew more frantic. "You have to help."

"Finley?" Crispin sounded as if he suspected the answer was yes.

But Edmund shook his head no.

"Who came?" Corbin pressed, his heart pounding. Edmund was shaking, his face pulled in absolute terror.

"Mr. Bentford," Edmund whispered, his voice breaking.

Corbin froze. *Mr. Bentford?* But Mr. Bentford was dead. Clara was a widow. Wasn't she? Frantically thinking back on it, he couldn't be certain he'd ever heard her say specifically that her husband was dead.

"He'll hurt Aunt Clara. He always hurts her."

He always hurts her.

Corbin took hold of Edmund and set him on Elf's back, joining him there in the next instant. "C'mon," he called to his brothers and set Elf at a run.

They were at Ivy Cottage in little more than a minute. Layton took charge of Edmund. Corbin, with Jason and Crispin on his heels, went through the front door without bothering to knock.

"You didn't really think you could get away with it, did you, Clara?" an unfamiliar voice said, something in the tone menacing.

"I have done nothing wrong," Clara answered.

Corbin heard panic and rushed into the sitting room.

She spotted him first. "Corbin," she cried out and rushed straight to him, throwing her arms around him.

Corbin wrapped an arm around her and surveyed the two men in the room. One appeared at least fifty years old, with weak, watery eyes and a hat with a terribly bent brim in his hands. The other man, however, was the one who kept Corbin's attention. He was younger than his companion, more finely attired, and watched Clara with a proprietary air Corbin found immediately offensive. But if he was, indeed, her husband, Corbin had no right to object. Still, he didn't let Clara go.

"Visitors, Clara?" the gentleman asked, smirking.

She pressed herself more firmly against Corbin. He sensed she was more than merely uncomfortable with the stranger; she was truly afraid.

"Corbin Jonquil." Corbin introduced himself without extending a hand.

"Robert Bentford." The gentleman returned the cold greeting and eyed the group assembled around Corbin and Clara. "And how do you know Clara?" he asked. Bentford apparently had a knack for making even the simplest of questions sound vaguely offensive.

"I am her neighbor," Corbin answered in a neutral voice.

"Friendly neighborhood." Bentford's lips twisted in obvious amusement, taking an exaggerated look at Corbin's arm wrapped around Clara.

"What precisely are *you* doing in the neighborhood?" Jason took over the questioning.

"Visiting my dear sister-in-law." Bentford grinned threateningly.

Sister-in-law. Corbin pulled Clara closer to him. The jack-a-napes was her late husband's brother. Corbin had never been more relieved in all his life.

"He's having me thrown in jail," Clara whispered.

"On what charges?" Jason had obviously heard.

"Assault," the older of the two gentlemen answered, obviously uncomfortable with the situation.

"Against whom?" Jason asked immediately.

The gentleman looked nervously at Bentford.

"You would bring charges against a lady?" Crispin asked Bentford. "Your own sister-in-law?"

"I don't believe I caught your name," Bentford drawled.

"I don't believe I offered it," Crispin replied smoothly. "I am assuming you are the one she supposedly beat within an inch of his life." Crispin looked him up and down in a condescending way that would have injured any man's ego.

"You jest, sir," Bentford said. "But I assure you, it was no minor thing. An incensed woman with a fire poker can do a great deal of damage."

"And what did you do to incense her?" Jason regained control of the interrogation.

"Nothing at all, I assure you," Bentford answered without batting an eyelash.

Clara's grasp on Corbin tightened. "Please don't leave me, Corbin," she whispered. "Please don't leave me."

He rubbed her back in long, slow circles, hoping to calm her and reassure her. He would never leave her to face such a horrid man alone.

"Hers was an unprovoked attack," the other gentleman said.

"And what is *your* interest in all this?" Jason asked.

"I am the squire," the man said, speaking with so much uncertainty the statement sounded almost like a question.

"And you are charged with returning her to the neighborhood where the alleged crime took place," Jason surmised. "How well do you know Mrs. Bentford?"

"Relatively well. She lived in Hamilton for three years."

"You believe Mrs. Bentford would cold-bloodedly attack a man without provocation?" Jason asked doubtfully.

"Well . . . I . . ." The squire began fiddling nervously with his hat brim and looked to Bentford as if for an answer.

"Hmm." Jason watched the exchange closely.

Corbin had seen enough. "Where's Alice?" he whispered to Clara.

"In her room."

"Edmund, take Layton to Alice's room," Corbin instructed. "Bring a doll and a blanket to take with her."

Layton and Edmund went upstairs immediately.

"You can take the girl anywhere you want," Bentford said, "but Clara is going back to Sussex."

"No." Corbin slipped Clara behind him. "Mrs. Bentford is coming home with me."

"I might have known you'd be handing out your favors," Bentford spat at Clara.

That was the last and final straw.

Corbin took a single step toward Mr. Bentford and punched him in the nose. The crunching sound proved eminently satisfying.

"Get out," Corbin growled at him.

"Not your house, Jonquil," Bentford snapped, holding his hand to his nose, a tremendous amount of blood pouring from it. His glare was acidic.

Corbin shuddered to think what the man might have done to Clara. "Not yours either," Corbin reminded him.

"She really cannot go with you," the squire insisted weakly. "I have to take her back."

"Would you be willing to release her into the custody of the Baron Cavratt?" Crispin spoke over the squire's protests.

"Lord Cavratt?" The squire's eyes seemed to bug from his head. "Certainly. I know him by reputation. Lord Cavratt is well respected and honorable and trustworthy and—"

"Flattered," Crispin interrupted dryly.

"You're he?" the Squire sputtered. "He's you? That is, you're—"

"Crispin Handle, the Right Honorable The Baron Cavratt." Crispin made a slight bow. "And I will take full responsibility for Mrs. Bentford until this mess can be straightened out."

"Yes, my lord. Of course, my lord."

"Reynolds, you dolt." Bentford spoke through the handkerchief he held to his bleeding nose. "You cannot simply—"

"Perhaps it would put your mind at ease to know that the gentleman who just went upstairs is the future Baron Farland, and these two gentlemen are brothers of the Earl of Lampton." Crispin spoke with an aristocratic air to his voice and countenance that would have impressed the Prince Regent himself. "And that their mother, the Dowager Countess of Lampton, is at Havenworth, as are Lady Cavratt and Lady Marion Jonquil, daughter of the late Marquess of Grenton. I am certain those honorable ladies will happily vouch for Mrs. Bentford's remaining at Havenworth."

"That is certainly enough for me," Squire Reynolds answered, obvious awe in his voice.

"Good," Jason said firmly. "Now I suggest Mr. Bentford take himself off. This is Mrs. Bentford's property, and he has no right to remain here without her consent."

"And what would you know about it?" Bentford snapped.

Corbin was glad to see him discomposed. He looked almost ridiculous, his entire front stained with blood.

"Jason Jonquil, barrister."

Bentford seemed momentarily taken aback. He recovered himself though. "So an earl, a baron, a barrister, and a pugilist." He eyed Corbin with the last word. "Quite a family."

Corbin moved closer to him and enjoyed seeing Bentford flinch. "Know this, Bentford. The Jonquils are not a family to be trifled with."

Bentford's eyes grew wide for a fraction of a moment. Corbin glared back.

"Ready, Corbin," Layton announced, arriving at the sitting room door, Edmund pale and nervous at his side. Alice was in Layton's arms, rubbing her eyes and looking around in confusion.

"Mister," she called out to Corbin and squirmed out of Layton's arms.

"No, Alice," Corbin said. "Stay where—" But she'd already begun to scamper across the floor.

Alice stopped suddenly. Her eyes grew wide. Corbin followed her gaze directly to Mr. Bentford. Alice suddenly screamed in a way Corbin had never heard. The piercing, constant wails were not sadness or pain but bone-deep fear.

"Alice." Corbin crossed immediately to her. Alice threw herself into him, precisely the way her mother had, still screaming as though her very life depended on someone hearing and finding her.

He held Alice more tightly, trying to prevent his mind from formulating reasons why Alice would be so terrified of Mr. Bentford. The possibilities were far too horrendous.

"Tell me, Squire Reynolds." Corbin turned to the wide-eyed man, barely keeping his temper in check. "Does this seem to you like the reaction a child would have to a man who had done 'nothing at all' to her mother?"

That seemed to have an impact.

Corbin kept Alice in his arms and returned to Clara's side. He could see she was trembling. He wrapped an arm around her waist. She leaned into him. He didn't flatter himself that she was reacting out of anything other than the need for his support. But she was in his arms, just the same.

"We have our own squire here," Corbin warned the unwelcome visitors. "He can see to it that you leave Ivy Cottage."

"Not necessary," Bentford said with mock civility. He was gone in the next moment.

"I am sorry, Mrs. Bentford," Squire Reynolds offered, hanging his head as he slipped out after Bentford.

Alice was still sobbing.

"Did he hurt Aunt Clara?" Edmund asked, suddenly standing in front of Corbin, looking up at him with worried eyes.

"No." Corbin did his best to reassure him. "And I won't let him."

Edmund's chin quivered, and he leaned against Corbin, his arms hanging at his side as if he were too exhausted to even lift them.

Corbin looked to his brothers, to Crispin. "I need you to help me," he said to them. "We can't let Bentford hurt this family."

"You said it yourself, Corbin," Jason replied. "The Jonquils are not a family to be trifled with."

"We aren't Jonquils," Edmund muttered from the level of Corbin's waistcoat.

Layton looked down at him. "You are. More than you know. Come on, Edmund. I'll sneak you into Havenworth before Caroline realizes you're there."

Corbin mouthed a thank you as Edmund wandered in Layton's direction. "Alice, dear." She was still crying in his arms. "We are going back to my house. Will you let Jason hold you?"

"Is Jason bad?" Alice asked, her words broken by her continued sobs.

"No. I promise you he is not bad. He is my brother."

Alice nodded and sniffled. Her trust touched him, especially in light of all he'd just seen. He handed Alice over to Jason, hoping their resemblance would put her at ease. She went willingly, though her tears continued.

Corbin turned to Clara. Tears pooled in her eyes, though they didn't fall. She, no doubt, held them back with a willpower she had been forced to call upon before.

He pulled her back into his arms and held her as she shuddered. It was improper, he knew, to hold her so closely when no one else remained in the room. But he didn't care. She needed him. And he needed her, needed to know she was safe and comforted.

"You didn't leave me," she whispered.

"Of course I didn't, Clara. Of course I didn't." Corbin held fast to her. "Everything will all . . . Everything will be fine."

"But Corbin"—her voice faltered—"they will put me in jail."

"No."

"I did what he said I did." She looked up at him, fear obvious in her eyes, tears threatening to fall at any moment. "He can prove that I did."

Chapter Seventeen

Not two steps out of the carriage after arriving at Havenworth, Edmund's legs seemed to give out. Clara rushed to his side, but Corbin was there in an instant. What would she have done throughout this ordeal without him? she thought. Corbin lifted the boy from the steps and carried him inside.

"He's going to hurt Aunt Clara," Edmund muttered, his words thick and slurred from exhaustion.

"No, he will not," Corbin said.

Clara stood still, thoughts of Mr. Bentford filling her mind. How had he found her? How would they escape this time?

Edmund had already collapsed. Alice was whimpering for Mister. Clara did not know how much longer she could hold back her tears. *I will not cry*, she told herself over and over. *I have to be strong.*

But again and again came the awful truth. Mr. Robert Bentford had found her, and she didn't know how she would escape.

"Come up to the library, Mrs. Bentford." Layton had come up behind her, slipping a hand under her elbow to assist her. She didn't cringe as she would have with every man she'd known before meeting Corbin's family. Something about these Jonquils was different. "A few more minutes of your time and then you can rest," he promised.

"Thank you," she said softly in reply.

Ahead of them, Crispin and Jason were deep in conversation, leading the way up the stairs to Corbin's library. Crispin looked back at one point and nodded reassuringly at her.

You are more a Jonquil than you know, Layton had said to Edmund. Did he realize how much she'd come to wish she were a part of this family? They were watching over her and her children, and for the first time in years, possibly in the course of her entire life, she felt, at least momentarily, safe.

But Mr. Bentford was in Grompton. He was there. Nearby. He had the power to destroy her and this new life she had made for herself.

"Why don't you sit a moment, Mrs. Bentford?" Layton suggested, leading her to a settee near the fireplace. "Corbin will want to be here, and I think Lady Marion needs to be as well."

"Your wife?" Clara asked, unsure why she was being involved.

"You will understand soon enough." He offered no further explanation.

Clara sat on the settee and took several deep breaths. Layton had joined Jason and Crispin at the desk. She didn't attempt to overhear their conversation. She did her utmost not to think of anything at all. She closed her eyes and waited, willing her tears to dry.

Around her, muffled conversations continued. She heard the door open and close more than once, footsteps crossing the room.

"She is spent, Jason." Clara recognized the dowager countess's voice. "Couldn't you allow her to sleep and discuss this in the morning?"

"Time is our most difficult obstacle right now, Mater. Mrs. Bentford can sleep all she wishes tomorrow, but we need to begin addressing this tonight."

"You make this sound very serious."

Clara didn't like the worry she heard in the dowager's voice.

"If Mr. Bentford pushes these charges, if he has any proof, this could be quite serious."

"I recognize that tone, Jason," the dowager countess said. "You are all barrister right now. I will leave you to it."

Clara heard the dowager leave the room.

"Mrs. Bentford?" That was Jason's voice.

Clara opened her eyes. They had all assembled. Layton and his wife, Lady Marion. Crispin. Jason. Corbin had returned as well. Clara felt herself redden. Had she actually thrown herself at him in the cottage? She had been overwhelmed with relief when he'd come through the door. She was certain no other person would have been as welcome at that moment as he had been.

He'd held her every bit as gently as she'd seen him hold Alice. It was a novel and wonderful experience. Such comfort his embrace had given her in that moment! She had felt safe despite being surrounded by threats and danger.

Now he was keeping his distance once more. She bit down her disappointment.

"I need to ask you a few questions," Jason said.

Clara nodded, recognizing, as the dowager had, the lawyer tone in his voice. She forced her mind to the present and listened.

"Mr. Bentford claims you beat him with a fire poker. Is that accurate?"

Clara clasped her hands in her lap. "Yes."

"Were you defending yourself?"

"Not precisely." She clutched her fingers more tightly. "He hadn't done anything yet. That time."

"What do you mean by 'that time'?"

Clara glanced at Corbin, then around the room. There were so many gentlemen she hardly knew. They were helping her, she reminded herself. She needed them to.

Everyone seemed to await her response. Clara really didn't want to talk about those horrible months after the younger Mr. Bentford had descended on Bentford Manor. She'd been attempting to forget everything about that place, about the brothers who'd lived there.

Clara took a deep breath. She would have to explain far more than the night she committed her "crime." "Mr. Bentford inherited Bentford Manor after the death of his brother, to whom I was married." Another breath was necessary. "He, however, did not come to reside there for nearly a year after inheriting. There is no dower house at Bentford Manor, only a wing set aside for the use of the family widows. Mr. Bentford, the one who was at Ivy Cottage today, made that arrangement . . . difficult for me."

"Difficult in what way?" Jason pressed.

Clara fidgeted, glancing around at the room full of people who only days earlier had been strangers to her. She still hardly knew them. And Corbin's opinion of her had only recently seemed to grow approving. There'd been a softening there lately. Would he turn on her now?

"Is this entirely necessary, Jason?" Corbin broke his silence for the first time since entering the library.

"It is excessively necessary."

She would have to tell them everything. Clara could no longer remain seated, a rush of agitated energy surging through her.

"My husband was a violent man," she said. "Alice, thank the heavens, wasn't old enough when he died to remember him. I know Edmund works very hard not to. The late Mr. Bentford once broke Edmund's arm in a fit of rage." Her heart still thudded at that horrible memory. "Most of his outbursts, though, were directed at me. I don't think a single day went by when he didn't strike me, often repeatedly. I thought when he passed we would finally have peace. But I discovered his brother is cut from the same cloth."

She took as deep a breath as her tense lungs would allow. "Once he established himself at Bentford Manor, we were in the same horrible state we were before. I did all I could to protect the children from his wrath, but what could I do? There was nowhere to hide, no true means of defending myself. I consulted a solicitor in a nearby town, but he regretfully informed me that the law does very little to protect a woman from the anger of her male relatives."

Clara glanced at Jason and saw confirmation in his face.

"Is there more?" Jason seemed to sense there was.

She nodded slowly. This was the more difficult part.

"Mr. Bentford became increasingly familiar." Clara wrung her hands as she paced. "He took it as his right to use my Christian name, to take my hand whenever he chose, to be far more affectionate and pointed in his regard. I attempted to discourage him, which only made him angrier. I never knew if my encounters with him would involve a beating or an inappropriate display of affection or both."

Clara felt ill at the retelling, reliving in her mind details she was leaving out of her explanation. Those encounters had made Mr. Finley all the more unbearable. She knew all too well what scurrilous men were capable of.

"What direction did his attentions take?" Jason asked.

"Jason—" Corbin objected.

"We must prove that she had reason to strike at him," Jason cut him off. "I am sorry, Mrs. Bentford, but it is necessary."

"I understand." Clara lowered herself onto the settee once more. "He eventually abandoned all semblance of propriety, speaking in ways that were not only uncomfortable but threatening. My continued rejections only increased his violence toward myself and the children. I threatened to speak to the squire, but Mr. Bentford was adamant that my word would never carry the weight his would. The law would, he warned, tell me to go back to the keeping of my male relatives and be grateful they were willing to let me stay on."

Clara swallowed back a sudden surge of bile. She could not look up, couldn't bear to see what might be written on the faces of those who had offered to be her champions.

"I tried to leave with the children once, but we were found out. He beat Edmund and Alice, beat them badly. I was too afraid to try again.

He said that should I so much as make the attempt, he would have guardianship of Alice taken from me and would send her to some cousin to be raised."

She took a shaky breath. Those months with her brother-in-law had been, by far, the worst of her life.

"I discovered through the help of a sympathetic and discreet man of business that so long as I was living at Bentford Manor, the estate received a stipend for my care, though we were living very much like paupers. Mr. Bentford was pocketing that money and, if the society column in the papers was to be believed, was using it to fund a gambling addiction. He needed us to remain because he needed the money. The beatings and the unwelcome attentions were all his way of terrifying me so much that I would be too afraid to leave."

She felt a warm tear slide down her cheek. She'd tried so hard to keep her tears at bay all evening. She swiped at the moisture on her face.

"He underestimated, however, my unwillingness to see the children continually beaten and tormented. I secured Ivy Cottage through this same man of business, of whom Mr. Bentford was not aware, and secretly packed the necessities for one more attempt at leaving."

Clara closed her eyes tightly to force back the tears that threatened. She was determined to finish her telling. She heard a rustle of skirts, then felt the settee shift beside her. Clara glanced over. Lady Marion sat next to her. Clara felt the young lady's arm wrap around her shoulders. A tear slipped out at that simple gesture. She never permitted herself to cry but couldn't seem to prevent herself now. She was entirely unraveling.

"We very nearly slipped out before Mr. Bentford came looking for us." Clara pressed on. "Suzie was taking the children to the carriage I had hired from a nearby inn, and I was gathering the last of our things. I heard Mr. Bentford in the moments before he entered my bedchamber. I grabbed the fire poker and hid beside the clothespress. He found me rather easily, but before he had a chance to say much more than good evening, I hit him. I hit him as hard as I could."

Lady Marion's arm squeezed her more tightly.

"That was when I saw his valet in the doorway. His valet is unfailingly loyal to Mr. Bentford and holds me in extreme dislike. He would, I am certain, testify that Mr. Bentford had done nothing upon entering to justify my attack."

"The law would place almost no confidence in your testimony if it contradicts his," Jason said.

"I fled the house." Clara rushed through the rest of the telling. "Mr. Bentford's valet shouted at me that I would hang for what I'd done. That was when we came to Ivy Cottage. We have been hiding from him ever since. And until this evening, I thought we'd managed to find a corner of the world quiet enough that he wouldn't look for us here. But he has, and now we'll never be safe from him again."

The room was silent. Clara wiped at a tear streaming down the side of her nose. Would they abandon her now? Did they even believe her?

"With a witness and, no doubt, the word of the local physician regarding his injuries, Mr. Bentford has a case," Jason said. "The penalty for assaulting a gentleman is steep. Transportation, if she is lucky."

Clara's shoulders sagged.

"You'll forgive me if this sounds impertinent." Lady Marion seemed to address the entire room at once. "If Mr. Bentford needs Mrs. Bentford to return home with him so he can secure a portion of her jointure, what benefit can he possibly expect at having her transported or imprisoned?"

"Not impertinent at all, dearest," Layton answered. "An insightful question, actually."

Clara's spinning mind hadn't allowed her to consider that possibility yet.

Jason's brow furrowed in deep contemplation. "I would have to look at the marriage settlement to know for certain, but I would guess that either a criminal conviction will strip Mrs. Bentford of her income, keeping all of it for the estate, or Mr. Bentford plans to offer to take her back into the family home rather than subject her and, I am certain he will insist, the family name to the degradation of transportation or imprisonment or worse."

Clara pushed out a tight breath. "So either his goal is to let the law do away with me or imprison me again himself in the home I only barely managed to escape?"

"I believe so."

She dropped her head into her hands. This was her nightmare, the very thing she'd feared the past six months. How hard she'd worked to stay hidden, to choose a place she thought Mr. Bentford wouldn't look for them. She'd done something almost unspeakably frightening in fleeing Bentford Manor. She'd gone out into the world alone to create a new life for herself. All that effort. All her hopes. Crumbling.

"Our best course of action is to prevent the case from being heard," Jason said.

"How do we do that?" Corbin asked.

There had to be a way. There simply had to be.

"How quickly can you dispatch an express to Philip?" Jason asked.

"As quickly as you can write it," Corbin said. "But . . . but I do not think he can leave Scotland yet."

"He doesn't have to leave," Jason said. "A letter from the Earl of Lampton should give the circuit judge second thoughts about the case presented to him."

"I'll write one as well," Crispin said. "And I am certain Lord Henley, my brother-in-law," he explained, apparently for Clara's benefit, "would add his voice."

"I see now my role in this," Lady Marion said from beside Clara. "I am assuming you wish me to send an express to my cousin, the Marquess of Grenton."

Jason nodded. "Precisely. And to the Duke of Hartley."

Clara snapped her head up. "The Duke of Hartley?"

"Do you know him?" Jason asked, studying her closely.

"Only as a passing acquaintance. He has a small estate in Sussex, not ten miles from Bentford Manor."

"Would he be acquainted with Mr. Bentford?"

"I think so, though I don't believe he approved of either Mr. Bentford."

"Perfect." Jason's look of confidence was remarkably reassuring.

Clara found herself breathing a little easier.

"I will write to Roderick this instant." Lady Marion rose from her seat and crossed to the desk.

"Will it be enough?" Corbin voiced the question Clara herself was silently asking.

"If His Grace will testify, even in writing, against Mr. Bentford's character, and Philip, Crispin, Henley, and Grenton will throw their weight behind a formal objection to the charges," Jason said, "there are few judges who would continue with the proceedings."

They were using rank and titles and influence, Clara realized. She had heard of such a thing but never imagined anyone doing so on her behalf, especially not a roomful of men. Why would they do that? She was nothing to them.

"Wouldn't our . . . knowing Mrs. Bentford has allies . . ." Corbin said to Jason. "Wouldn't that alone be enough for Mr. Bentford to not pursue the charges?"

"It might," Jason said.

"It won't." Clara heard a tremor in her voice. Every face in the room turned to her again. "He doesn't like to be thwarted. He is arrogant and proud and—" She took a breath, trying to calm herself. "He would continue to try simply because he has been humiliated. Because he has lost, he will feel he has to prove he can win. And even if that weren't enough, he needs the money. From all I could gather, he needs it desperately."

"Horrid man," Lady Marion muttered.

"I will write to Lord Devereaux as well," Crispin said with a look of determination. "He has some influence at King's Bench and might be able to put a little fear into whomever is conducting the assizes in Sussex next month."

A flurry of activity erupted: quills flying across parchment, servants being instructed to prepare the fastest mounts in the Havenworth stables. Most of the express missives would be sent to London, which simplified the campaign. Catherine entered in the midst of the flurry.

"Mater has set out tea in the sitting room," she said quietly to Clara. "She is convinced the boys are starving you up here."

The boys. Clara looked around the room at Crispin and the Jonquils. There was far too much drive and power in the room for her to possibly think of them as *the boys.*

Her gaze settled on Corbin. *Dear Corbin.* He'd come to her rescue. He'd held her tenderly. Now he and his brothers were attempting to save her once more.

"They are a force to be reckoned with, aren't they?" Catherine looked around with obvious familial affection. The Jonquils, it seemed, had adopted Catherine as one of their own.

"They are writing to the people they know who have the most influence," Clara explained, feeling herself blush beneath her pallor. She didn't feel worthy of their efforts but didn't dare object. They were, possibly quite literally, saving her life. "They hope it will be enough to have the charges against me dropped."

Catherine crossed to where her husband was writing a letter. "Crispin, dear."

"Yes, love?" he replied without looking up.

"To whom are you writing?"

"Devereaux," he answered, continuing to write.

"You really ought to write to the Duke of Kielder."

The entire room grew instantly silent, all eyes turning to Crispin. Even Clara had heard of the Duke of Kielder. He was legendary. His influence was limitless; even the uppermost levels of society stood in awe of the duke. No one contradicted him. No one dared earn his wrath. It was said he could command the kingdom with a single snap of his fingers.

"You know the Duke of Kielder?" Jason asked, awe in his voice.

Clara had never heard Jason sound impressed.

"We have worked together on several bills in Lords."

"Would he add his weight to this?" Jason asked.

A smile spread across Crispin's face. "I think he would."

"No one gainsays the Duke of Kielder," Catherine said.

"I have told you before, Crispin," Jason said. "Your wife is a genius."

Catherine colored prettily. Crispin kissed her quite unabashedly and then quickly finished his letter and began another.

"Mrs. Bentford." Jason turned to Clara. "I believe you may rest easy now. It seems you are to have the entire House of Lords on your side."

Chapter Eighteen

Corbin felt entirely useless. He had little interaction with the aristocracy or the influential in society. His brothers were going to save Clara. He was grateful for that, more than he could possibly say, but he wished he could do more.

Only willpower and his brothers' continuing insistence that beating the life out of Robert Bentford would not help Clara's precarious situation kept Corbin from hunting down the dog. No wonder Clara never spoke of her past. Everything she *had* told them occurred *after* her husband had died. Edmund described the late Mr. Bentford as a monster. The rogue had broken the boy's arm. Broken his arm!

The letters had been dispatched. Jason himself had left for London. Crispin and Catherine would follow in the morning. Crispin had written to the Duke of Kielder—the charges would never stand if Kielder spoke against them. Layton and Marion had sent word to Grenton and Hartley.

Everyone had helped except for him, and it was *his* family that was in trouble—they felt like his family, Clara and the children.

The children. Corbin would forever be haunted by the sheer terror he'd heard in Alice's cry when she'd caught sight of Mr. Bentford. He needed to check on them, be sure they were resting and unafraid.

Catherine had whisked Clara from the library nearly two hours earlier, no doubt at Mater's insistence. Clara had looked terribly pale and worn. Corbin hoped Mater had seen to it that Clara had something to eat and went to bed. He would have suggested it himself, but he'd needed to dispatch the letters necessary to ensure her freedom.

Corbin climbed the stairs to the nursery wing.

Edmund had said his stomach ached when Corbin had left him with Caroline's nursemaid. No doubt he was ill from worry and tension. He hoped Edmund was feeling better. He hoped Alice had stopped crying. He hoped Clara would allow him to hold her again.

Corbin could still remember how she'd felt in his arms, as if she was made to be there. *His other half.* He'd let her go very reluctantly, knowing he'd likely never have another opportunity to hold her.

He knew which room in the nursery wing Edmund had been given and crossed directly to it. A light burned inside. He stepped through the doorway. Edmund was sleeping, curled in a ball on his side on the bed. In a chair very near him sat Clara, Alice asleep in her arms.

Corbin stood still and quiet, taking in the scene. It was the closest he'd ever come to seeing perfection.

The illusion dissolved at the sound of a muffled sob, one he knew did not belong to either of the children.

"Clara?"

She looked up at him, and he saw tears streaming down her face. Pain pierced him at the sight of her hurting like she was. Even in the retelling of her encounters with Robert Bentford, she hadn't cried so openly, without any effort to control her emotions. Corbin crossed to where she sat and gently took Alice from her arms. He laid the girl on the bed beside Edmund, careful not to wake her as he slipped the blanket around her as well.

Clara hadn't risen when Corbin turned back toward her. He held his hand out to her, wondering if she would accept it. He'd been less than heroic during her ordeal, letting his brothers undertake the rescue efforts. She might very well have written him off as useless.

She hesitated only a moment before placing her hand in his and allowing him to help her to her feet. Holding her hand, he discovered, was not nearly enough. He wiped the moisture from her cheeks with the heel of his hand. She closed her eyes. She was still too pale, her eyes red-rimmed from prolonged crying.

"What can I do, Clara?" Corbin asked, desperate to be useful.

She looked up at him, anguish in her eyes.

Corbin slipped his hand from hers and cupped her face. He'd never kissed a woman before, something most gentlemen would never admit to. He'd often wondered if, when the opportunity arose, he would even know what to do. But in that moment, instinct simply took over.

He gently pressed his lips to hers, holding her face in his hands. Slowly, gently, he kissed her, breathing in the sweet scent of her. Every thought fled from his mind, every sound silenced. He was aware of nothing but her.

His hand slid from her face to her shoulders, then down her back, his arms wrapping around her and holding her close. Clara didn't pull back, didn't object. He felt her grasp his waistcoat as she kissed him in return.

"Mister?"

Clara broke away first, though she didn't flee his embrace. Corbin was certain he was as red as a strawberry.

"Yes, Alice?" He kept his arms around Clara as he glanced at her daughter.

She still appeared half asleep. "Kisses for me too?" She held her arms up in an obvious request.

If he hadn't been red before, Corbin certainly was then. *Kisses too.* Obviously, they'd had an audience.

He met Clara's gaze. She gave him a small, tremulous smile.

He moved to the bed, hunching down beside Alice, and kissed her forehead. "Good night, sweetheart," Corbin whispered.

"G'night, Mister." She curled up beside Edmund.

Corbin smoothed back her hair, watching her for a brief moment. She seemed to have recovered to some degree from her earlier ordeal. He hoped Edmund had as well.

Corbin rose and turned to Clara. She was no longer there.

"Clara?" he quietly called after her, not wanting to disturb the children. She wasn't outside the door in the schoolroom.

Had she fled from him? Certainly his kiss hadn't been so unwanted, so unpleasant. No. She had returned the gesture and, as far as his inexperience could ascertain, had enjoyed it. Corbin's heart sank. She'd had a difficult evening. She'd been tired and upset. Had he taken advantage of that? Had he pressed unwanted attentions on her?

Corbin closed his eyes and leaned against a wall of the nursery, hoping he hadn't ruined everything with that kiss, a kiss he knew he would never forget.

* * *

More than a moment passed after Clara awoke the next morning before she realized where she was. The events of the evening before rushed over her. She was tempted to simply crawl under the blanket again and pretend it was all a horrible dream.

You are no helpless hothouse flower, wilting at the first difficulty. She had set out on her own and saved herself and her children—at least temporarily—from her brother-in-law. She would not sit by helplessly when there was a problem to be addressed. The Jonquils were helping her. She didn't know their reasons, but she was grateful for all they'd done. She would, she vowed, help them in any way she could.

She sat up, her head faintly aching from a night of weeping. She walked barefooted across the cool, wood floor to a dressing table. Her eyes were a little puffy but far better than she would have anticipated.

"Are you awake, then?" a voice asked from the doorway.

Clara looked over to see a servant girl, probably no more than sixteen or seventeen years old, smiling kindly at her.

"Mr. Jonquil had your things sent over this morning." The girl crossed to the clothespress and opened the doors. Her clothes, probably very nearly all of them, hung neatly inside.

Clara crossed to the clothespress herself and opened the drawers. Her underthings and stockings sat inside.

"The children?" she asked quietly.

"Their things as well," the girl confirmed. "Mr. Jonquil said you would want your things here. 'Specially the children's. 'Twould make them feel more at home."

"It certainly will," Clara said.

"Now, what would you like to wear today? I'm to be your maid, if you've no objection."

"None whatsoever." She hadn't had a lady's maid since Mr. Bentford's death. "What's your name?"

"Fanny," the girl answered.

Fanny? Why did that sound familiar?

"Thank you, Fanny."

An hour later, Clara made her way through the long corridors of Havenworth, having broken her fast in her room and looking, in her opinion, better than she had in some time.

She felt inexplicably nervous. Would she come across Corbin? Would he be indifferent, stiff and disapproving? Would he be sympathetic and gentle? She couldn't possibly predict. Clara knew she would probably blush the moment she saw him, remembering, as she had all night and all morning, that lovely and unnerving kiss. She'd realized as she'd stood in his embrace, kissing him and being kissed in return, that she'd fallen in love with him. And it frightened her.

"You cannot say anything to anyone, Caroline." That was Charlie; Clara was certain of it.

"But I saw you driving Corbo's carriage."

Clara reached a bend in the corridor and spied Charlie and Caroline facing one another with equally defiant expressions. Clara kept to the corner, out of sight.

"I was only putting the carriage back," Charlie insisted. "And the scratch was already there."

"You scratched it?" Caroline's eyes grew wide. Apparently, even at her young age, she understood the significance of that misdeed.

"It wasn't my fault. And you cannot tell Corbin."

Charlie forever seemed to be in some kind of mischief. Clara had heard of a broken window and a shattered vase. Edmund had spoken more than once of Charlie disrupting the stable hands and making more work for them.

Not wanting to find herself in the midst of another of Charlie's larks, Clara stepped inside the sitting room.

"Mrs. Bentford." The dowager countess sat on a sofa embroidering but was looking up now that Clara had entered. "How are you feeling this morning? What a horrible day you had yesterday."

Clara nodded. The dowager motioned for her to join her on the sofa. She sat and waited, unsure what would come next.

"A Squire Reynolds was here this morning," the dowager informed her.

Clara closed her eyes, forcing a slow breath.

"He was quite easily persuaded to return to Sussex. It seems he is remarkably impressed with our Crispin." She sounded as though she was holding back a laugh. "I suppose I would have completely ruined the effect if I had told the squire about the time Crispin and Philip got their breeches stuck in the back garden gate at the Park. My husband laughed for fifteen minutes without hardly stopping for breath at the time."

Clara smiled at that, the first smile she'd managed since Mr. Bentford had entered Ivy Cottage the evening before. She looked at the dowager. "How old were they?"

"Thirteen." The dowager chuckled at the memory.

"Philip is your eldest?" Clara asked. There were a lot of Jonquils, and she couldn't quite keep them all straight.

"Yes," the dowager answered fondly. "He is in Scotland just now."

"Yes, Corbin said so last night." Clara remembered hearing as much.

The dowager nodded, a look of concern once more etched in her features. "Philip took Sorrel, his new bride, to Scotland to see a surgeon. She was injured many years ago and walks with a profound limp. This surgeon thought he might be able to help her. The surgery, I understand, went well, but Sorrel is not recovering quickly."

"I hope that doesn't mean she is suffering any serious complications."

"So do I." The dowager sighed. "Philip's last letter indicated she was experiencing a tremendous amount of pain but that the surgeon believes her leg will heal well."

"Philip seems to be a very attentive husband," Clara said. Was there yet another Jonquil who was gentle and kind? It was almost unfathomable.

"Sorrel has been very good for him." The dowager sighed again. "She has sobered him in ways he needed. And Lady Marion has lightened Layton, who has a tendency to be too sober. They have both chosen well for themselves. But I worry for Corbin."

The dowager was intent on her embroidery once more and couldn't possibly know the discomfort her words caused Clara.

"He has always been painfully shy," the dowager continued. "Few ladies would be willing or able to see past that. Even with his own family, Corbin is terribly quiet."

Shy? She'd never thought of Corbin as shy.

The dowager continued stitching. "Philip took Corbin to Town for the Season—oh, it must have been three, perhaps four years ago. Corbin has a great deal to recommend himself. He is wealthy enough to support a family in style. He is good-natured, well mannered, and would be a faithful and loving husband. Yet the moment he was in society, at a ball, a dinner, a musicale, he would freeze up, his tongue tying in knots. The poor man couldn't speak a word to anyone. More than one person, I am afraid, came away convinced our Corbin was arrogant, which, I assure you, is as far from the truth as possible."

Clara looked away, her mind churning. *Couldn't speak a word to anyone. Arrogant.* She thought back on all of the interactions she'd had with Corbin, the myriad times he'd seemed unhappy in her presence, unimpressed and distant, cold even. Could he simply have been uncomfortable because he was shy?

"Corbin hardly speaks to his own family, let alone strangers," the dowager added. "Philip could not convince Corbin to return for the next Season. He has seemed a little better these past couple of weeks. He doesn't stammer as much as he once did. That dear boy. I hope he can overcome his timidity enough to catch some lady's eye."

Clara bit down on her lips, thinking. *Shy*? No, she shook off the thought. He hadn't seemed at all shy last evening with Mr. Bentford. He'd tossed him out of her house after threatening him rather eloquently and, she remembered with some satisfaction, very likely breaking his nose.

And timidity certainly hadn't factored into his kiss.

She closed her eyes and thought of that kiss. Somehow, he'd touched her soul with that simple, lingering gesture. She'd lost her heart to the gentle and considerate side of him. If the disapproval she'd seen was indeed simply shyness . . . With a surge of welcome hope, Clara tucked the possibility away.

"Your Edmund is a sweet little boy," the dowager said.

"He is that." The love she felt for her nephew had grown and deepened over the years he'd been in her care. She thought of him like her own son. What would she do if Mr. Bentford carried his point? She couldn't subject Edmund to that life again.

"Corbin has enjoyed having Edmund as his little shadow in the stables." The dowager smiled fondly. "The way he describes the boy's love of horses reminds me of Corbin as a child. Such a hard worker. Such a tender heart."

Corbin and Edmund did have a special bond. Clara had seen it many times over. And Alice had fallen so fully in love with her mister all those weeks ago when she'd first seen him behind them at church.

A thought rushed through her mind in that moment. She'd been at loose ends searching for a way to assist in her family's rescue. She might not have had any ability to save herself, but she knew she could help the children.

You can take the girl anywhere you like, Mr. Bentford had said of Alice. He had no interest in the children. Should the unthinkable happen to her, she could at least be sure her children were safe and happy.

Chapter Nineteen

Clara took a portable writing desk out to the back gardens of Havenworth. It was a peaceful and quiet place, something she welcomed after the upheaval of the past few days. She hoped Corbin's family and their lofty associates could clear her name. But even if they managed to solve her legal difficulties, it would hardly free her of the crushing weight she carried.

She would never be truly free of Mr. Bentford so long as he knew where she was. She would have to run again, find another tiny hamlet in which to hide.

Poor Edmund. What will he do without Corbin and the horses? He'll be heartbroken. And Alice has grown so attached to Corbin as well. I cannot pull them away from the first kind and caring man either of them has ever known.

If she uprooted the children so often, neither of them would ever form any lasting friendships. How would Alice ever hope to marry if she never stayed in a neighborhood long enough to be courted? Edmund might manage to make friends once at Eton.

Clara stared down at the blank parchment in front of her, her heart growing heavier by the moment. Could she truly do what she was contemplating? Could she sacrifice so much for the sake of her children?

So long as Mr. Bentford needed her widow's jointure, he would never leave her be. And to have his scheme crushed as decisively as the Jonquils were planning would be a blow to his pride he wouldn't soon forget. She would never be truly free of him. She would likely spend the rest of her days running and hiding.

But I cannot subject the children to that kind of life.

Trouble hadn't sunk her yet; she wouldn't allow it to now. Should Corbin's family be unsuccessful and she be imprisoned, transported, or hanged, she simply needed to have a plan in place for the children. Even if she were forced to return to Bentford Manor, she would not make the children return there as well.

Corbin, she felt certain, would allow Edmund and Alice to stay at Havenworth. Edmund could earn his keep helping in the stables. When Alice was old enough, she too could find a means of being helpful. And Corbin would be kind to them. That meant more than almost anything else.

Sweet, kind Corbin. His gentleness had assuaged so many of her fears over the past weeks. He was the first man she'd truly trusted and depended on. Her man of business in London had proven himself reliable, but she still preferred him at a distance, as she did all men. But Corbin . . . Corbin was different.

He has always been painfully shy. She had pondered the dowager's declaration many times over and could see the first hints of truth to it. She had seen him color on occasion. And he most certainly stammered and stumbled over his words. There did seem to be a thread of timidity running through him.

Clara bent over her portable writing desk and began writing out instructions. She gave the name and direction of her man of business. She listed the amount of Edmund's inheritance and how she wished it be used. She made a list of the names of Edmund's relatives on his father's side, warning of their unsuitability. Corbin would need these details written out for reference.

After the ink had a chance to dry, Clara pulled out a second sheet of paper. She would need to write out instructions to her man of business to transfer the keeping of Edmund's inheritance to Corbin while explaining her continued need for secrecy in her whereabouts.

"I heard rumors the Jonquils had taken on another pet project." Mr. Finley's voice cut into her moment of determination, leaving her unsettled and nervous again. "I didn't realize you were their latest stray."

There he stood but a few paces ahead, leaning quite casually against the thick trunk of a tall tree.

"I do not believe Mr. Jonquil wishes you to be on his land," Clara said calmly. She slipped her papers back in the desk.

He simply gave her an overly confident smile. "Are they rallying to your cause, Clara?"

She held her chin high. Past experience had taught her that correcting his use of her Christian name would do no good. "I bid you good day,

Mr. Finley." She stood and began walking with as much confidence as she could muster.

Even with her long strides, Mr. Finley caught up to her in the shortest of moments. "Let me guess. The Jonquils took up the challenge of ridding you of your bothersome relative without so much as a second thought, without waiting to be asked?"

She didn't at all like that he knew exactly how her rescue had played out. She avoided his question with one of her own. "How do you know about my 'bothersome relative'?"

"Everyone knows, Clara."

Everyone knows. She would indeed have to move. There was no other way to be rid of Mr. Bentford.

"And everyone knows the Jonquils have taken you under their wing." Mr. Finley's tone wasn't happy on her behalf but commiserative, as though having a family such as theirs championing her was reason to feel sorry for her. "I knew them when we were children, you realize."

She had guessed as much. The mutual dislike she'd sensed in Corbin and Mr. Finley oozed with history and past interactions. But she didn't ask for an explanation. She simply continued on toward Havenworth, hoping Mr. Finley would leave her be.

"They were forever collecting strays and nursing wounded animals," Mr. Finley continued, easily keeping pace with her. "As adults, they graduated to the care of less-fortunate human beings, rallying to some valiant cause or another. But, Clara, dear, the moment they've finished playing the hero, the Jonquils return to their own. They may be willing to undertake some charitable feat or another, but they do have their level."

"What do you mean?" She asked the question, though she felt certain she already knew the answer.

He stepped in front of her, forcing her to stop walking. His look was both sympathetic and somehow proprietary. "They are willing to help you, to rally behind someone less fortunate. But, Clara, they come from a long line of titles and distinction. You can be quite certain they realize you do not. They took in a great many strays over the years, but their stables only housed the finest animals. They have taken up a great many causes but have admitted only their *equals* into their family circle."

She shook her head. The picture he painted didn't match the kindness she'd seen in the Jonquils. It most certainly didn't match Corbin's loving and kind heart.

"I am only warning you so you won't be hurt," he insisted. "Think on it. Layton Jonquil, who will be a baron in his own right one day, married the daughter of a marquess. A *marquess*. Philip, the earl, married a lady whose intimate circle of friends included a duke's sister-in-law and a lady who married a very well-respected title. The only friend they have ever considered as close as family is a baron who rubs elbows with the Duke of Kielder."

All of that was inarguably true. She herself had felt out of place among them all.

"If you have set your heart on being adopted by them, you will only be disappointed, my dear."

His words hit their mark. She had begun to think of herself as part of their circle. But she refused to let him see the disappointment she felt bubbling inside. "What concern is it of yours?"

He reached out as if to touch her face. She stepped immediately out of his reach. No man had the right to touch her without her consent. No man.

He only smiled. "I know they have vilified me. Tearing down my reputation has been a particular goal of theirs for years."

"You have torn down your own reputation, Mr. Finley," she said firmly. "You reveal your character time and again by ignoring the repeated rejections of the women you relentlessly pursue."

"I only pursue those with enough fire to make my efforts worthwhile. I enjoy a challenge, you see." He stepped closer. "I could give you a future, Clara. Some security to see you through these difficult years ahead of you."

She scoffed at that. "I doubt even you would stoop so low as to marry a penniless widow with no connections."

"Marry you?" He laughed humorlessly. "Come now. I may not have been born to the same lofty heights as the Jonquils and their associates, but I think you know perfectly well I wasn't proposing marriage."

Despite the sick feeling settling in her stomach, Clara eyed him with resolve. "I may not aspire to the level of the aristocracy, but I assure you, sir, neither will I stoop to the level of a snake."

She pushed past him, walking faster than ever.

"This is not over between us, Clara," he called after her. "I like a challenge, and I do not give up easily."

Here was yet another man who would never leave her be. Not even in the temporary sanctuary she'd been granted at Havenworth could she feel more than a moment's peace. Running and hiding, worrying and fear seemed destined to be her lifelong companions.

She reentered the house, and a few moments later, she came across the butler. "Would you inform Mr. Jonquil that Mr. Finley is currently on the Havenworth grounds? I believe he would like to know."

The butler gave a single nod before leaving to deliver the message. Even the Jonquil servants felt more lofty than hers ever had. Though she dismissed most of Mr. Finley's words, she couldn't shake the truth of his very lowering reminder: the Jonquil family was rallying behind her, Corbin even seemed to genuinely care about her, but there was no denying she was not their equal. Titles married titles. The wealthy reserved their inner circles for their fellow wealthy.

She might have been their latest stray, their latest charitable endeavor, but in the end, she could really never be anything but that. Despite that lowering realization, she clung to her faith in Corbin. He would be good to her children; she was certain of that. She was depending on it.

Chapter Twenty

In the two-and-a-half days Clara had been at Havenworth, Corbin had hardly seen her and not once since he'd kissed her. The closest he'd come was a message relayed to him through his butler that Finley was on his property. He'd attempted to speak to Clara about it directly, to make certain Finley hadn't frightened or imposed upon her, but she had retreated to her bedchamber, where no true gentleman could go.

Edmund and Alice, on the other hand, seemed unwilling to be parted from him. Edmund shadowed him all over the house and stables. Echoes of "Mister!" rang through the halls of Havenworth with regularity. But Clara remained elusive.

It seemed he'd offended her with his kiss. Perhaps he'd done it wrong. Perhaps he was simply no good at it. He didn't want to think about the obvious answer, that she didn't return his feelings.

He'd thought almost constantly of what it would be like to kiss her again, to hear her say she cared for him.

"Corbin?" Edmund sat at the desk in the library, reading. He had begun calling him Corbin in the last twenty-four hours, a change that warmed Corbin's very heart. How he loved these dear little children. And they seemed to be learning to care for him as well. "What does C-I-V-I-L spell?"

"Civil," Corbin answered quietly, not wanting to wake Alice, who was asleep on his lap. He stroked her tiny head, hoping she would continue to sleep. The children's nurse said Alice had not slept well, waking up at night, apparently from nightmares. Clara, he was told, had spent the last night in Alice's room.

"What does *civil* mean?" Edmund asked.

"Civil means acting polite and well mannered."

"Then a civil war is a war fought politely?" Edmund asked, genuinely confused.

Corbin smiled. "No. A civil war is a war fought within a country."

"Oh." Edmund returned to his reading. He was a conscientious student, Corbin had discovered, keeping to his studies even though he was not at home and his aunt Clara was not pushing him to do so. He would do well when he went to school.

"Mister?"

"Yes, Alice?"

She sounded groggy still. He hoped she would drift back to sleep.

"Bad man gone?"

"Yes, dear. The bad man is gone."

"Mister?"

"Yes, Alice?"

"I can stay here?"

"You may stay here as long as you'd like." Corbin pulled her closer to him, resting his cheek on the top of her hair.

"And Mama?" Alice asked.

"She may stay as well."

"Ebum?" That, Corbin knew, was the closest Alice could come to saying Edmund's name.

"Edmund as well."

"Mister?"

"Yes, Alice?"

"I love Mister."

Corbin kissed the top of her head. "I love you, Alice."

"And Ebum?"

"Yes, dear." Corbin looked over at Edmund, who watched him intently. "I love Edmund too."

Edmund smiled. Corbin motioned him over. Edmund climbed onto his lap beside Alice and buried his face in Corbin's lapel.

"Love Mama?" Alice continued her questioning.

"Yes," Corbin whispered. "Especially Mama."

Alice grew heavy against him, sleeping once more.

"Is Mr. Bentford truly gone?" Edmund asked after a moment passed.

"I do not know where he is, Edmund. But you and Alice and your aunt Clara are safe here. I promise you that."

"Did you hit him?" Edmund asked. "He was bleeding."

"I did hit him."

"Why?"

"He said something—something to your aunt Clara that he shouldn't have."

"Something mean?"

Corbin couldn't think of what Bentford had said to Clara without tensing. To imply, as he had, that she was a woman of loose morals . . . He couldn't countenance it. "What he said was very mean."

"What if he said something mean about Alice? Would you hit him?"

"Hitting isn't always the right answer." Corbin again remembered the lesson his father had taught him on that very topic. "But I wouldn't allow him to hurt any of you."

"Aunt Clara is afraid," Edmund said. "I saw her in Alice's room this morning. She was crying again. She only cries when she is afraid. I think she thinks Mr. Bentford will come back."

Corbin processed that. Clara was still worried. He wanted Clara to feel safe at Havenworth, to feel at ease, at home. He wanted her to want to stay.

Jason had written only that morning to say he and Crispin would be meeting with Lords Henley and Devereaux and the Dukes of Hartley and Kielder to discuss Clara's situation. He further wrote that he fully expected to receive letters from Philip and the Marquess of Grenton, who were the only gentlemen on the list not currently in Town. The wait was excruciating.

In the meantime, there had to be something Corbin could do to keep Clara's mind off her troubles. He had never been good at planning entertainments or social events. He would need to think about it.

"Corbin?"

"Yes, Edmund?"

"Is it babyish to be afraid? Does it mean I'm not very grown-up?"

"Even very grown-up people can be afraid," Corbin assured him. "Are you afraid?"

"Mr. Bentford is mean." Edmund shifted his position until he fit under Corbin's right arm. "He hit me sometimes. And it hurt a lot. The other Mr. Bentford did too. He broke my arm. I don't want this Mr. Bentford to break my arm."

Corbin took a few deep breaths to steady his anger. No child should have to endure what these two had. Corbin held Edmund as tightly as he dared.

"He hit Aunt Clara too and made her bleed. He did that all the time. Every day."

"My brothers and I will take care of Mr. Bentford, Edmund. You do not need to worry about him."

"I like your brothers," Edmund said, his eyes now closed. "And your mother says I can call her Grandmother. I thought that was nice."

Corbin smiled. "Very nice." *And optimistic*, he thought silently. A little manipulative too, he suspected.

Edmund didn't offer any more comments. Corbin realized rather quickly that the boy had fallen asleep. Edmund and Alice were both sleeping in his arms. He took a deep breath and closed his eyes. He may not have slain Clara's dragons for her, but he felt, at that moment, like he was making a difference.

He'd told Alice the truth. He loved them more than he'd ever thought possible. And he loved Clara, almost desperately. Her smile had captured him early on, and since that time, he'd discovered she was witty, kind, brave, and loving. She had a good heart. He loved her all the more for it.

* * *

Clara walked the halls of Havenworth, hoping to find Corbin. She needed to talk to him about the children. She peeked only briefly through the open library door but didn't step inside. The room was quiet and still.

Then, a tiny, nasalized sigh sounded from inside. Clara felt certain it was Alice's baby snores. She followed the sound all the way to a chair set beneath the far windows, turned away from the door. She stepped around the chair, and the sight she discovered left her nearly breathless. Corbin sat with Alice asleep on one side of his lap and Edmund asleep on the other.

Corbin smiled at her a little awkwardly, the slightest hint of color stealing across his face. *Shy*, his mother had called him. Only a few short days earlier, she would have interpreted his stiff demeanor and half smile as disapproval.

"They fell asleep like this," Corbin said quietly. "I am trying very hard not to wake them."

"However did you get them to sleep?" Clara asked.

Corbin didn't answer immediately. "I think they . . . that they were just tired."

It was more than that, Clara knew. They'd been tired the night before, but she hadn't been able to get them to sleep for more than a short while at a time. They were worried, tense, fearful. She hadn't managed to assuage their fears, being too bogged down by worry herself.

Clara stood silently watching the three of them, hesitating to blink for fear she would miss the perfect picture laid out before her. No one but herself had ever loved these children.

That was why she was searching for him. Corbin loved her children, and he would take care of them.

"What is it?" Corbin interrupted her thoughts.

She focused on him again. He looked back at her, concerned. Something of her thoughts must have been visible on her face. Clara shook her head, her courage suddenly abandoning her. She couldn't possibly ask more of him.

Clara turned away, her heart pulsing, her mind racing. Behind her, she could hear movement, fabric rustling and shifting.

She turned back. Corbin was rising from his seat.

"Please don't wake them. They've hardly slept these past few days."

"They won't wake," he answered assuredly.

He gently laid Edmund back on the chair, his head on one armrest, his body curled in a ball on the seat. Corbin held Alice against his shoulder. He carried her to a nearby sofa and laid her softly on it. Neither child had awakened.

"Now." Corbin returned to where Clara stood speechless. "What is weighing on you?"

Clara shook her head.

Corbin interrupted her nonverbal denial. "I can see it in your eyes, Clara."

Until Corbin had begun calling her Clara, she had never truly liked her Christian name. Somehow, Corbin made it sound almost poetic.

"Please tell me." Corbin took her hand and held it comfortingly.

Her gaze was riveted to Corbin's hand, much the way it had been at church nearly a week earlier. His was so much larger than her own and yet so gentle.

"Jason will write to tell us about the meeting today," he said.

The meeting. Suppose the Lords and Dukes refused to help her? Suppose they, rightly so, felt their time was too valuable to waste on someone as unimportant as she was? What would she do? What would happen to Edmund? To Alice? Tears stung the back of her eyes, her stomach tying in more knots.

"You're crying," Corbin said.

"I'm not crying." Clara wiped at the lone tear that had managed to escape. "Not very much," she amended, frustrated that she couldn't keep her emotions in check as she usually did.

"Edmund told me you . . . told me you only cry when you are afraid."

That brought further tears. A boy Edmund's age ought not to have to worry as he did.

"What is it you are afraid of?" Corbin took hold of her other hand.

"What if this plan doesn't work?" She stopped for a shaky breath. "What if Mr. Bentford carries his point?"

Corbin looked genuinely concerned. Because he didn't think his family could save her? Because she was worried? She ought to ask him, ought to plead with him. Her own emotional upheaval did not help.

Clara pulled away and stepped back to the window, resting her hands on the sill. "The late Mr. Bentford never shared custody of Edmund with me. I was his sole guardian, which is unusual for a woman." She knew she was most likely completely confusing Corbin, but if she was going to ask what she needed to ask, Corbin had to understand the circumstances. "He has no other guardian, no one to take him should something happen to me. My brothers were specifically barred in Edmund's parents' will from being made his guardians."

There was nothing but silence behind her. Clara's first inclination was to assume Corbin was indifferent or annoyed at her for dumping at his feet her personal difficulties. *He is shy*, she reminded herself. *And quiet. It is simply his way.* And, she realized, she liked that about him, now that she was beginning to understand him.

"The late Mr. Bentford was quite clear from the first day of our marriage that he would never acknowledge any child of mine who was not male." Clara quickly continued her tale, paling at difficult memories and, yet, blushing at the personal nature of the topic. "So Alice was legally disowned by him. She has no claim on his estate. She is unacknowledged by his family and always will be. A loophole in the marriage settlements gave her the right to remain with me at Bentford Manor, but there is nothing else the Bentfords can or will do for her."

Clara grasped almost desperately at the window sill. How she hated reliving the years she'd spent under the tyranny of the Bentford family. Was it any wonder she'd so naturally assumed the worst about Corbin?

"If something were to happen to me, there would be no one to care for my children." Clara rushed through the words. "They would find themselves in a poorhouse or an orphan asylum." She was crying in earnest now, her worst fears verbalized.

Corbin came and stood beside her at the window, facing her. "Clara." Though he spoke her name quietly, something in his tone made her shiver, not with fear or apprehension but at the tone of authority she heard in his voice. "Do you truly believe I would allow Edmund and Alice to be sent to any such place?"

"I hoped not," she whispered without looking up at him. "But I couldn't ask you—"

"You didn't have to," he replied.

She believed him. Immediately. "If . . . if I am forced to return to Bentford Manor, I cannot take the children, Corbin. I know what he'll do to them. I know the pain he will happily and repeatedly subject them to."

"Them and you," Corbin reminded her.

She swallowed the lump in her throat. "Yes. But if I can save them from that, I can endure it myself. Can they stay here with you if I am forced from Ivy Cottage?" She couldn't phrase the question as *when* she was forced to leave, though she knew that would be more accurate.

"I . . . We won't allow that to happen, Clara." He took her hand once more. "Whatever it takes, we'll fix this."

She couldn't manage a reply. "Thank you again for not abandoning me to all of this. No one has ever stood by me before. No one has ever cared what happened to me."

"Someone cares now, Clara." His look was so intent she couldn't help but believe him.

She joined her free hand with the one he held, clasping his hand between hers. The children were sleeping, their world for once peaceful and safe. What would she have done without Corbin in their lives? He had stood by her, supported her through the past days.

Though he had never said he loved her, never expressed that sentiment, she knew he cared. She cherished that, treasured it. Their disparate state might prevent anything greater from coming out of it, but she would cherish the connection they did have.

"Do you ride?" he asked unexpectedly.

She turned to look at him. "Horses?"

He chuckled lightly. "Yes, horses." His blue eyes sparkled when he smiled. Corbin was ridiculously handsome with a smile on his face.

She managed a half smile of her own, wiping a lone tear with her hand. "I haven't ridden since we left Bentford Manor."

"Do you have a riding habit?"

Clara nodded. "Provided it was brought over from Ivy Cottage."

"I am certain it was." He still hadn't released her hand, and she wasn't fighting to be freed. "I am . . . There is . . . You—"

He stopped suddenly, a hint of color tinting his face. He was flustered.

Heavens, Clara thought, *he* is *shy. Why did I never see it before?*

He was muttering to himself as he often did when stumbling over words. Again, she wondered how she'd missed that connection. She'd always assumed he was telling himself how displeased he was. But that wasn't it at all. He only did that after fumbling over his words. It was clearly his way of regaining his composure. How could she have been so blind?

"There is a mare in the stables I think you would . . . would enjoy riding." He took another breath. "She's well trained. And Elf would appreciate a ride too."

"Elf is your mount," Clara said, remembering Edmund telling her so several times.

"I . . . Will you ride with me?"

She heard the uncertainty in his voice as he made the request, and her heart jumped inside her. All this time, he really had simply been shy. She'd misinterpreted his aloofness. That lightened her heart in a way nothing else could have.

"What about the children?" Clara asked.

"We can take them to the nursery." He seemed anxious for her reply.

She nodded her agreement. "A ride would be splendid."

Chapter Twenty-One

An orphan asylum? The poor house? Did Clara really think him so heartless as to allow the children to go to any such place? The memory of those words haunted Corbin as he waited at the front door for Clara.

She'd spoken as if convinced she'd be hanged or transported. Corbin clenched and unclenched his fists. He wouldn't allow it. He would take Clara out of the country if he had to.

It was no wonder she'd looked so painfully tired. With such a weight on her shoulders, she likely wasn't sleeping. He probably ought to have insisted she go to her room and rest instead of accompanying him on a ride. But he couldn't help thinking she needed distraction every bit as much as she needed rest.

The children had hardly stirred when they'd laid them on their beds in the nursery. A nap would do them good. The two would, with any luck, begin sleeping through the night once more, which meant Clara might too.

"It is still creased, I am afraid." Clara interrupted his thoughts as she came hurrying down the stairs, smoothing the front of her riding habit. "I haven't laid it out in more than a year."

She was a vision. The green of her riding habit brought a reddish hue to her hair and made her emerald eyes all the more vivid. Her hurried descent had brought a hint of color back to her cheeks. For the first time since Mr. Bentford's arrival in Nottinghamshire, Clara didn't look burdened.

Riding had been a very good idea.

Corbin motioned for her to precede him through the door. Outside, the sun shone, and a light breeze ruffled the lawn and trees. It was a wonderful day for a ride. Clara smiled at him, and the day was suddenly perfect. She seemed more comfortable with him than she had ever been before. He would need to tread lightly, be careful not to overstep himself.

"I hope this mare is not too docile," Clara said. "I have not had a good, bruising ride since I was a schoolgirl."

"A bruising ride?" Corbin raised his eyebrows. Somehow, he couldn't picture her riding neck-or-nothing. "You want a dangerous mount?"

"Do you have a horse that is dangerous?" Clara asked, interest evident in her eyes.

Corbin nodded. "Devil's Advocate. Philip's mount."

"The great black one?"

Corbin nodded. How had she known that? They hadn't reached the stables yet.

"Edmund is in awe of a great black horse that he, apparently, sees with regularity here."

"That would be the dangerous one." Corbin smiled. "Only Philip and I have ever ridden him. *Successfully* ridden him."

"Then I have no desire to make the attempt," Clara assured him.

Corbin came to a sudden conclusion. "Whipster." She looked up at him in obvious confusion. "A stallion," he said. "He's more than . . . He has more than a decade behind him but still has some fire left. Though not so much that he'll unseat you."

"That sounds perfect."

They reached Whipster's stall quickly. The horse was all but retired now, reserved for the occasional jaunt about Havenworth.

"He is beautiful." Clara watched the roan, which stood still and peaceful.

"My father gave him to me," Corbin said. "About three years before he died. He was only . . . Whipster was only a colt then."

"So you raised him?"

Corbin nodded. The Lampton Park grooms had done most of the raising, as he was still at Eton. But the horse had been Corbin's responsibility, one he'd taken very seriously.

"And now you have an enormous stable full of horses to raise." Clara's gaze followed the long line of stalls. "Edmund would love such a thing."

"And he would do a fine job of it," Corbin answered. "He has been a joy to have here. He works hard, and he loves the animals."

Clara rubbed Whipster's nose, clearly taking to the old stallion. "I cannot thank you enough for allowing Edmund to work here. Knowing you has changed him—for the better."

The praise brought a blush to Corbin's face. He wondered if he'd ever outgrow that tendency. At twenty-six, it didn't seem likely.

"Do you want me to saddle Elf, Mr. Jonquil?" Jim asked, stepping up to the stall.

"Yes, and a sidesaddle for Whipster."

Jim nodded and fetched the saddles.

"You are a sweet one, aren't you?" Clara cooed to Whipster. The old stallion nickered in response. Clara smiled adoringly.

"Whipster likes you," Corbin said.

She turned that same smile on him. "And I like him. I like him very much."

Corbin had always dreamed of finding a lady who loved horses. Watching Clara gently interact with the one animal in the stables that meant the most to him, Corbin lost a little more of his heart to her.

A few minutes later, Jim returned to guide Whipster from his stall. Clara walked alongside Corbin but watched the animal she'd come to adore so quickly. Corbin could easily grow used to moments like this one. Clara at his side.

They reached the paddock, and Jim quickly saddled Whipster. The stable hands had neglected to bring a mounting block for Clara, and Corbin glanced expectantly at Jim. The man smiled back at him, grinned, really. It took but a moment to understand he was being conspired against, though the staff likely thought they were plotting *with* him. There was but one way for a lady to mount her horse without a block—someone had to assist her.

He cleared his throat, willing his face not to redden further as he turned to face Clara. "It seems the staff has neglected your mounting block."

She glanced in the direction the block ought to have been, then returned her gaze to him. "They are likely not accustomed to needing one. I do not imagine you ride out with many ladies." Her expression seemed to almost freeze as an unmistakable hesitancy entered her eyes. "Do you?" she asked. "Ride with many ladies?"

The redness he had feared a moment earlier threatened to erupt at any moment. He shook his head but did not answer out loud. Other than Mater, he had never ridden with any lady.

A blush touched Clara's cheeks. Corbin thought he saw relief in her features. Though she'd fled from him after that unforgettable kiss, he could not help thinking now that she was not so very indifferent to him. "I can send the staff for a block. Or—" He swallowed against a sudden lump. "Or I can assist you."

He wasn't sure which answer he hoped for or dreaded more. If she allowed his assistance, he'd be permitted to touch her again. Happy as such a circumstance would be, he'd probably shake like a leaf. But if she refused his offer, he'd not be able to explain away her decision as anything but a rejection. He stood quite still and waited.

"I have not ridden in some time," she said, giving no hint as to her inclination. "I'm as likely as not to fall right back off."

Though she affected a light tone, Corbin detected a little nervousness beneath the words. "I'll not let you fall," he assured her.

She watched him intently as if searching for something. The fear he'd heard in her voice earlier when she'd spoken about the children's fate struck him anew. Life had obviously taught her not to depend on anyone, least of all a man. Even mounting a horse seemed a nerve-racking exercise in trust.

"I promise you," Corbin said, "I'll not let you be hurt." He hoped she understood he referred to more than merely helping her into her saddle.

"Sometimes that cannot be prevented," she said, her tone heavy. "All we can do is hide and hope the danger doesn't find us."

She referred to Mr. Bentford, he would wager. She had been hiding from him, and just as she said, he had found her.

Corbin stepped closer, desperate to know how he might wipe the worry from her eyes. She didn't back away from him. He took her hand in his, the simple touch setting his heart pounding. He knew he ought to say something, but he'd never been one for words. So he stood there with her hand in his, unsure if she understood what he wished he could convey.

Whipster nudged Clara's shoulder with his nose. She glanced quickly at the horse, then gave Corbin an uncertain smile. "I believe he is growing impatient with us."

Corbin nodded.

"You wouldn't mind helping me up?" she asked.

"Not at all." Even the simple phrase proved difficult to produce.

He cupped his hands for her foot and gently but firmly gave her the needed lift. While she situated and balanced herself, Corbin remained at Whipster's side, determined to be there should Clara need him.

Clara breathed something of a sigh of relief. She looked around her, a hint of a contented smile creeping across her face. "A moment or two in motion and I believe I shall quite have the knack of it again."

Corbin mounted as well, and they set off at a leisurely pace. He watched Clara as they rode. Despite her earlier concerns, she showed no signs of being ill at ease. She sat her horse with a natural grace and agility. Perhaps they might undertake a swifter pace before the ride was over. He had always found a cathartic release in letting his horse have its head and feeling the rush of wind against his face.

At the moment though, he simply enjoyed her company. She did not speak much, commenting now and then on the scenery or on Whipster. Corbin offered little beyond a word or two in response, something that did not seem to bother her. She didn't push him to rattle on and on as Harold had suggested he do, nor to heavy-handedly direct their outing as Jason might have suggested. Neither did she object to his subdued choice of riding attire. He felt peaceful with her as they rode, not constantly wondering if he ought to be or act differently than simply who he was.

They ambled across the back grounds, far from the noise of the stables. Before Clara had moved to Ivy Cottage, this had been Corbin's favorite place at Havenworth. Upon her arrival, it took second place to the copse of trees that led to her home.

"I am afraid I would get little done if I had a horse as fine and a view as tempting as this." Clara sighed, looking around her.

Corbin would give her all the horses she wished and free rein of the entire property in an instant. He wanted nothing more than to have her at Havenworth. He'd realized in the brief moments he'd thought Clara's *husband* had come to Ivy Cottage just how desperately he wanted her to be his wife, that he would give anything to have her with him always. But he couldn't simply say that. The words would never come out whole. Neither could he say with any certainty how his admission would be received. He thought she cared for him, perhaps even harbored some tender feelings. But could she grow to love him, the rather useless Jonquil? He doubted it.

"Corbin!" Clara's voice was urgent but whispered.

He followed her wide-eyed stare. Not one hundred yards ahead of them was a man on a coffee-brown mount. Corbin recognized him after less than a moment—Robert Bentford—and he was making his way toward them.

"Corbin." Her voice had turned pleading.

"I won't let him hurt you, Clara." Corbin sidled up so he and Elf stood between her and the approaching man.

"I knew he wouldn't give up. I knew it," Clara muttered.

When Bentford drew near enough to hear without Corbin raising his voice, Corbin calmly, authoritatively said, "Get off my land, Bentford."

"Clara." Bentford ignored Corbin. "There is no point hiding here. The trial can be held without you, though I wouldn't recommend it. Judges look harshly on criminals who do not attend their own trial."

"I am not a criminal."

"Make it easier on yourself and come with me." Bentford spoke with all the trustworthiness of a snake. "I am certain we can work this out."

There was an insinuation in Bentford's tone that made Corbin's blood pound in his veins.

Bentford moved his mount closer. "Clara. You know—"

The man ceased his comments at precisely the same moment Corbin pulled his pistol. All the brothers had decided that being armed would be a good idea so long as Bentford remained in the vicinity.

"Get off my land," Corbin repeated slowly so each word was punctuated. He wasn't pointing his weapon; he was simply holding it in a way that proved he knew how to use it.

"You plan to hang alongside her?" Bentford spat.

"For shooting a man trespassing on my property and threatening my guest?"

"I wasn't threatening—"

"That would be difficult to prove if you are dead."

Bentford pulled his mount back. "This isn't over, Jonquil," he hissed.

"It could be over in a flash, Bentford." Corbin's heart pounded. He'd never shot a man before. He didn't want to and was counting on Bentford being unwilling to call his bluff. Were Clara in immediate danger he would, of course, do whatever was necessary for her safety. Corbin sincerely hoped it didn't come to that.

"You cannot hide forever, Clara," Bentford said in parting. In less than a minute, he had disappeared.

Corbin put away his weapon, breathing a silent sigh of relief.

"He will never leave me be." Clara's voice shook. "I will spend the rest of my life running from him."

Corbin silently vowed he wouldn't let that happen.

Chapter Twenty-Two

Corbin received a letter from Jason that evening. He read it several times, assuring himself he had not misread the missive. He gave it to Clara after dinner and watched her as she read it, knowing what it contained. She read it aloud, as the rest of the family was not privy to its contents.

Corbin,

The meeting with Lords Devereaux and Henley and the Dukes of Hartley and Kielder went well. All are willing to back Mrs. Bentford against Mr. Robert Bentford.

The Duke of Hartley proved especially helpful. He does, in fact, know Mr. Robert Bentford and possesses information which would prove damaging to that man's character and would most likely bring down upon him his creditors.

Lord Devereaux has identified the judge who will be in Sussex for the assizes, and he, along with Crispin and Lord Henley, in possession of the letters we only just received from the Marquess of Grenton and Philip, will visit him personally tomorrow morning.

Please tell Mrs. Bentford not to worry. The charges will, without a doubt, be dismissed.

Yours, etc.

Jason

Clara seemed to be reading the letter again. Corbin watched, wanting to see the worry disappear from her eyes. He'd hoped their ride would have had that effect. But thanks to Robert Bentford, it had not. She had, at least, joined the family for dinner, something she'd not yet done since coming to Havenworth. Corbin took that as a good sign.

"He seems very confident," she said weakly.

"Jason knows what he's about," Layton reassured her, standing nearby as well. "If he says the charges will be dropped, they will be."

Clara's gaze locked with Corbin's. He could easily read in her eyes the question she didn't speak out loud. She wanted to believe Jason was correct, desperately wanted to, but had known too much disappointment to let herself feel relief. He gave her a firm nod.

Suddenly, Clara's face went unearthly pale.

"Clara?" he whispered urgently, crossing immediately to her. She leaned against him, still staring at the letter.

"I won't have to stand trial? I'm not facing transportation or . . . or anything?" Her words were oddly halted, as though her brain and mouth weren't fully communicating with one another.

"No," Corbin replied. "All of those worries are behind you."

She took an audible breath. Her arms dropped to her sides, her strength obviously spent. Corbin kept an arm around her, wishing he could do more. Clara pressed her open hand against his chest, resting ever more of her weight against him.

"She needs to rest, Corbin," Mater said. "You'd best take her to her room."

"Mater." Corbin felt his face burn with embarrassment. Accompanying a lady to her bedchamber was not within the realm of acceptable behavior for a bachelor.

Mater just chuckled. "I had planned to go with you, son."

Corbin exchanged a brief glance with Clara, asking silently her opinion on Mater's instructions.

"I am more than a little worn down," Clara said. "I probably should rest."

He walked slowly down the corridor, simply enjoying her closeness and the rare moment of being the one to help rather than the one watching uselessly. He felt Clara shift beside him and, without warning, press a brief kiss to his jaw. Heat stole up his neck and over his face. She was too close not to notice.

"Thank you, Corbin," she whispered, leaning her head against his shoulder. "I couldn't have endured this without you."

"It has been my absolute pleasure," he answered.

They reached Clara's bedchamber. True to her word, Mater accompanied them inside, though she kept a distance.

"Try to rest," Corbin said. "You no longer need to be concerned about Mr. Bentford."

But she didn't look the least relieved. Worry clouded her eyes.

"What is it, Clara?"

She gave a small shake of her head. "He won't stop simply because he can no longer use the law to get what he wants. He said it himself just today. He'll find me. No matter where I go, he'll find me."

She spoke as though she meant to "go" somewhere very soon. "Are you leaving?" he asked, his heart dropping at the words.

"So long as I stay here, he'll not give anyone a moment's peace. Not me, not the children. Not even you." A resigned determination crossed her features. "But you promised to look after my children. You promised to take care of them."

"Clara." He did not at all like the direction this conversation was taking.

"Mr. Bentford has no interest in Edmund or Alice, except as a means of punishing me. He'll leave them be if I am not with them. He'll spend his time and energy looking for me. They could have a safe and happy life."

"Clara." He took both her arms in his hands, locking his gaze with hers. "You are . . . Are you honestly thinking of . . . of leaving the children?" Not only the children, but she was talking about leaving *him* too.

"I don't know what else to do." Tension pulled at her features and pinched her words. "Mr. Bentford knows I'm here. And being on your land didn't keep him away. He was here today; you saw him."

"He was forced to leave," Corbin reminded her.

"Because you were with me. What if you aren't the next time? What if he snatches one of the children to force my hand?"

Corbin's heart pounded ever harder. He understood the source of her fear. He couldn't think of any arguments that would nullify her worries. If Mr. Bentford needed the money from her jointure so badly, he likely would be willing to snatch her away, with or without the blessing of the law. What risk was there to him in doing it? He was her closest male relative. Few people would side against him in family matters.

"I cannot stay here and put the lives of the people I care about in danger. Neither can I ask the children to live their lives as nomads, always looking over their shoulders, afraid of their own shadows." Her shoulders squared. Her expression cleared. "Until I can be certain Mr. Bentford will leave me be, I have to do what is best for my children."

"Is there nothing I can say to make . . . to convince you to stay?"

"I can't."

There were no words after that, nothing Corbin could force his mouth to formulate. She didn't feel safe with him. She didn't feel that she could stay. She trusted him enough to care for her children but couldn't bring herself to believe in him more than that.

He gave her a quick, awkward good-bye and quitted the room.

"That poor young lady," Mater said once the door was shut behind them. "She has obviously had a difficult life."

Corbin nodded. *Difficult* seemed too tame a word. An abusive husband, a father who seemed much the same, a brother-in-law who beat her, imposed upon her, and was now attempting to have her punished for protecting herself from him, whose underhanded methods were forcing her to leave behind her own children. If only Corbin knew how to set her at ease, how to save her from the cruel hand fate had dealt her.

Mater linked her arm with his, and they began walking. "I have watched you, Corbin, since coming for this visit. You are in love with her."

There was no point denying it. Mater had always been able to read him like a book—she had that ability with all of the brothers, in fact.

"And?" Mater prodded.

"She . . ." *Thinks I'm an idiot. Doesn't know I exist.* No. He didn't think she thought of him that way any longer. "She doesn't feel the same way."

"Why do you think that?"

"I . . . I tried. I tried being fashionable and making an impression that way. And I . . . I tried to seem more assertive. That didn't work. The family even . . . even forced me onto her pew. But she—" He shook his head in frustration. "She is grateful to me, but I can't seem to . . . Nothing I do—" He wasn't sure how to finish the thought. Clara didn't love him or trust him enough to stay with him.

"Oh, Corbin." Mater stopped him in the middle of the corridor, squeezing his arm. "Being something you are not isn't the way to win a woman's affections."

"Being *me* doesn't seem to be the way either."

"If Clara Bentford does not love you, Corbin Lucas Jonquil, precisely as you are, then she is not the lady for you, my dear." Mater gently patted his cheek.

But I want her to be. I want her to love me. He remained silent.

"So stop listening to your brothers."

"How did—?"

She lightly laughed and explained. "No one but Philip would suggest you needed to be flamboyantly fashionable. And Jason, I would guess, suggested being assertive. Harold would tell you to quote holy writ day in and day out, which would get tedious. Layton would have, at one time, told you there was no point trying. Charlie would most likely shrug and ask if you wanted to go for a ride. And Stanley, well, I'm not sure he would have any advice. All he managed to do once he met a young lady who captured his attention was play backgammon with her. I love your brothers dearly, but they aren't very bright."

Corbin actually smiled despite the weight on his heart.

"Sorrel fell in love with Philip only *after* he stopped acting the part of a mindless dandy. Marion fell for Layton only *after* he let down his defensive wall. It was only after they stopped trying to be something they weren't that they won their fair maidens."

"What if—" He took a steadying breath. "What if Clara never—" He shook his head. *What if she truly leaves me?*

Mater smiled her understanding. "Let us deal with that if it happens. And let us hope that it doesn't."

Corbin managed a half smile. Mater was generally optimistic, but he found himself hard-pressed to match her. Clara was running scared, and he was losing her. Nothing he could think of would change the reasons for her flight. Mr. Bentford *would* likely continue to harass her if he knew where she was. She was going to leave, and Corbin's heart would never recover.

I won't let that happen, he silently vowed. *No matter how many people I have to talk to, no matter how many favors I have to call in. Somehow, someway, I won't allow this to happen to her.*

Chapter Twenty-Three

Clara, with the help of Suzie and Fanny, spent a few days packing her things at Ivy Cottage while the children were busy at Havenworth. She hadn't yet decided how to break the news of her departure to Alice or Edmund. How could she possibly make them understand why she had to leave? Would they grow to hate her for it? She hoped not. She hoped someday they would look back and realize the necessity of it.

Perhaps she could visit Edmund at Eton if she was very careful about it. Years down the road when Alice made her debut, Clara could take a house in London for the Season and watch from a distance.

Pain radiated through her every time she thought of leaving them. She would miss so much of their lives. But what else could she do? She couldn't put them in danger. So long as Mr. Bentford was looking for her, she would never be entirely safe. If the children were with her, they would be in danger as well.

Leaving them would be the hardest thing she'd ever done, but she needed to find the strength to do it.

Corbin arrived at the cottage at precisely the time he'd promised, just as he had the last two days. The cottage was nearly empty, all of Clara's belongings in crates and barrels. She kept the children's things separate so they could be taken to Havenworth when the time was right.

Corbin had sent the letter she wrote to her man of business in London a couple of days earlier, along with a letter he himself was sending to Town. She expected to hear back within the week. Mr. Clark knew of several houses to let in various small hamlets throughout the countryside. He could find her something hidden away.

Fanny and Suzie climbed into the carriage waiting in front of Ivy Cottage. Corbin followed Clara inside, sitting beside her just as he had each day he'd brought her back to Havenworth. She had been grateful that he didn't make her walk. Every day Mr. Bentford could be seen on horseback following their carriage up the path leading away from Ivy Cottage. It was the same reason Corbin sent a groomsmen or stable hand to the cottage while she was there.

Though they hadn't discussed the threat of Mr. Bentford's continued presence, the reality of it hung in the air between Corbin and her. She knew he didn't like that she was leaving. She didn't particularly like it herself. But there was nothing else to be done.

The carriage rolled along the path toward Havenworth. As always, Clara caught sight of Mr. Bentford watching her go by. She refused to allow her worry to show but kept her posture upright and confident. He rode alongside the carriage, keeping pace with them.

Mr. Bentford was always somewhere nearby during the day. The Havenworth stable hands had reported that he returned to the inn in Grompton each evening and didn't come back until after breakfast. When she did finally make good her escape, she would have to do so in the dark of night or the earliest hours of morning.

Corbin's fingers wrapped around hers, holding her hand in a silent show of support. How she would miss him when they were apart. He was an anchor, a sure foundation she needed desperately. If only she had the power to see Mr. Bentford out of her life for good. But even Corbin, the son of an earl, with his lofty connections and associates, couldn't manage that.

She clung to his hand, grateful for the support she felt from him. In moments like these, she appreciated ever more his quiet strength. Without words, he showed her he cared, he cherished her, he wanted her to be happy and safe. If only she could be certain that was even possible.

Corbin raised her hand to his lips and pressed a light kiss to her knuckles. He had only recently begun doing that. Clara loved it. Adored it. The understated nature of that gesture fit him so perfectly. He didn't need to be flashy or showy. He was simply perfect the way he was.

He pulled her arm through his. Clara leaned her head on his shoulder, letting her eyes wander again to the window and Mr. Bentford framed there.

"I wish there was a way to be rid of him. If only he would leave me alone . . ." She let the thought linger unfinished. Corbin knew what she was thinking—she knew he did.

"Somehow or another, we will manage it, Clara," Corbin said. "We'll find a way."

"You haven't given up on me, then?"

"Never," he whispered, his breath rustling the hair near her ear. He was the only man she'd ever known who could come that close to her and cause her not an ounce of worry.

The carriage rolled through the gate at Havenworth. Two very large stable hands stood there waiting, a daily occurrence of late. Mr. Bentford knew better than to press his luck. He rode off down the road, leaving Clara at peace for the moment. She squeezed Corbin's fingers, silently communicating her gratitude. It was not a permanent solution to her troubles with her brother-in-law, but it was a momentary respite.

The carriage pulled up under the portico at the front of the house. Suzie and Fanny stepped out and made their way around to the servants' entrance. Corbin handed Clara out. Once he had exited the carriage, he took her arm immediately, walking at her side as naturally as if they were a lady and gentleman out for a leisurely stroll. She couldn't help but smile at remembering how ill at ease they'd once been with each other.

"It is good to see you smile again," Corbin said.

"I suppose I haven't had much reason to of late."

"Do not give up hope too soon," Corbin said. "I haven't . . . I don't intend to let him win by default."

"And we have a few days at least before I have to go." She tried to sound encouraging. "My man of business won't be able to respond to my letter for a while. We can be together until then."

He didn't answer. He simply continued walking with her past the entry hall and toward the sitting room. His family hadn't left Havenworth yet. Clara had grown quite fond of Mater and Corbin's brothers. She would miss them as well when she left.

If only I could know Mr. Bentford would leave us in peace.

Alice and Edmund were in the sitting room, along with Caroline, listening to Lady Marion read a picture book. Edmund smiled at them but quickly returned to the story. Alice, however, climbed down from Lady Marion's lap and hurried across the room.

Corbin lifted her up in his free arm, all the while guiding Clara to an empty sofa. She sat there and smiled when he sat directly beside her. Alice settled onto his lap, twisting his cravat about and looking happier than Clara ever remembered her being.

"I am afraid you will never have another neatly tied cravat with Alice here." Clara rested her head on Corbin's shoulder.

"My valet will likely quit trying." Corbin's tone was light and teasing.

Without warning, tears gathered in Clara's eyes. She knew their source. For days she'd been mourning the loss of this man and the joy she felt simply being near him, as well as enduring the heart-wrenching knowledge that she was losing her children. Life was, at times, horribly unfair.

Alice's eyes met hers, and worry settled in their depths. She could not burden her children with the worries hovering on the horizon. She managed a smile, but Alice didn't seem to believe it. She slid from Corbin's lap to Clara's and wrapped her tiny arms around Clara. Clara returned the gesture. Corbin held them both in his comforting embrace.

"You must think I am a terrible coward," she said to him. "All I ever seem to do is run away."

"Nonsense. I have never known your equal for bravery, Clara. I doubt I ever will."

She sat in his arms, holding her baby, missing already the fleeting taste she'd had of family and companionship and safety. It would be taken from her all too soon.

Chapter Twenty-Four

Clara had missed the entire Sunday sermon. Mr. Bentford had sat in a pew that had afforded an unimpeded view of where Clara had been sitting. Alice had seen him within minutes of his arrival and had instantly begun screaming.

Clara's only consolation as she'd taken Alice outside so as not to interrupt the service was that the child's repeated declaration of "Bad Man" while pointing at Mr. Bentford and shrieking as though she were being tortured had turned the entire congregation's disapproving notice on Clara's despised brother-in-law. She'd actually walked out more slowly than she might have otherwise.

But she was certain, as she stood outside the chapel doors rocking Alice in her arms, he would find a way to pass off the entire thing without it reflecting badly on himself. Shaking off the blame for his many wrongdoings was one of Mr. Bentford's talents.

Alice had calmed over the twenty minutes they'd spent in the churchyard, though she still occasionally muttered "bad." Clara's mind remained on Mr. Bentford. His continued residence in the neighborhood only confirmed her worries. He might not have carried his point with the law, but that wouldn't stop him from making her life miserable all on his own. As soon as she heard from her man of business, she would have to leave. There was no other way of saving Alice and Edmund from him.

She kept turning to an unfamiliar and exquisitely grand traveling carriage stopped very near the gates of the churchyard. It had pulled to a stop precisely there about ten minutes after Clara left the chapel, and though no one had exited, the carriage remained. She couldn't seem to keep herself from looking at it, for it was far finer than any carriage she'd ever seen and bore what appeared to be an ancient coat of arms emblazoned on the door and two heraldic flags shuffling in the breeze on either side of the liveried driver.

The sound of footfalls echoed from inside the chapel, and Clara retreated to a quieter corner of the churchyard, not wishing to be trampled as the congregation exited. Alice had finally drifted off to sleep. The girl, to Clara's discomfort, had grown larger of late and heavier.

Clara watched the worshipers as they filed out the chapel doors, and she kept a wary eye out for Mr. Bentford. She saw him the instant he stepped into the sunlight. Her stomach turned inside her, her head pounding anew. She would keep an eye on him and keep out of his reach.

"Clara," Corbin said, startling her. "I believe you . . . you may want a good vantage point for this."

Clara looked back at him, intrigued. Corbin nodded toward the crowd. "I have invited someone."

Clara let her gaze shift toward the gathering. The traveling carriage she had been admiring now stood with its door open. Crispin stood outside as if he'd only just alighted.

"Lord Cavratt?" she asked as Corbin took Alice. Her arms ached from the weight of the sleeping child. How had Corbin known that?

"Yes, but not only him. That is not Crispin's carriage," Corbin said significantly.

Who had Corbin invited? And why was this visitor so significant?

"Clara." A hand grasped her upper arm, even as the identity of the speaker sank in. Her brother-in-law never lost an opportunity to make his presence in her life known.

"Try not to be annoying for a moment or two, will you, Bentford?" Crispin had arrived at her side, looking at Mr. Bentford like one might look at a flattened spider. "His Grace wishes to be introduced to Mrs. Bentford."

Mr. Bentford dropped her arm and sputtered for a moment. Clara kept her mouth firmly shut, or she might have sputtered as well. *His Grace?* There was a duke present? One who wished to make her acquaintance? She'd barely managed to maintain her countenance when being introduced to the Dowager Countess of Lampton and Lord and Lady Cavratt. But a duke? She knew herself to be drastically far beneath the notice of a duke.

Clara glanced at Corbin. He offered a small smile and nodded minutely.

"Trust me," he said quietly.

She allowed herself to be led toward the spot where every eye in the crowd was focused. A man, the duke, she could only assume, stood quite uncaring about the attention he attracted. He was not as tall as the Jonquil brothers—they were exceptionally tall—but he was built on such a solid scale that he was immediately and entirely physically overpowering. The look on his face could only possibly be achieved by a man who was equally endowed with superior rank, intellect, and strength. As if this was not enough, he also bore a scar equally as menacing as his other attributes, running the length of his jaw and across his cheek and spider-webbing in between. All he required was a sword and a rolling sea to be the very picture of a pirate.

Crispin stepped forward. "Mrs. Bentford, may I introduce to you His Grace, the Duke of Kielder."

A mutter rumbled through the crowd. Clara felt what little confidence she possessed dissipate. This was the Duke of Kielder: fearless fighter of duels, undisputed last word in all quarrels and on all issues, the man who intimidated everyone from fishmonger to the prime minister to the Regent himself. He was rumored to have bested Gentleman Jackson with a single blow, shot the pistols out of two gentlemen's hands during duels, taken down a gang of notorious highwaymen unaided. If only a handful of the tales surrounding this imposing gentleman were true, he was not a man to be taken lightly.

Corbin had invited the most powerful man in the kingdom? Invited him to apparently meet her?

"Your Grace, this is Mrs. Clara Bentford, late of Sussex, who now resides in this neighborhood at Ivy Cottage."

The Duke of Kielder offered a gracious and very proper bow. Clara returned the acknowledgment with her deepest curtsy.

"I am pleased to make your acquaintance, Mrs. Bentford," the Duke said. "Next time you are in Town, I hope you will call on Her Grace and me. We would be very pleased to receive you."

Clara wasn't sure if she actually managed a response—she was too shocked to be certain.

"Now, Cavratt." His Grace turned to Corbin. "Where's the weasel?"

That sent another murmur through the crowd.

"This is he," Corbin said, indicating Mr. Bentford with a quick jerk of his thumb.

"You, sir." The Duke pointed over Clara's shoulder. "I would speak with you." It was worded very nearly as a request, but no one hearing His Grace speak would have mistaken it for one.

From behind Clara, Mr. Bentford stepped into the clearing the crowd had left all around their exalted visitor. "Your Grace," Mr. Bentford said, his tone nervous, his bow awkward.

The Duke looked down his nose. "Did I give you leave to address me?" he asked in a menacingly quiet voice.

Mr. Bentford shook his head. Clara had never seen either of the Mr. Bentfords so thoroughly intimidated.

"I am come with a message from the Duke of Hartley." His Grace's eyes narrowed in obvious dislike of the man he addressed. The crowd's attention eagerly shifted between the two men. "He wishes you to be told of a rather damaging piece of financial information recently revealed to your creditors. They, who I understand are quite numerous, ought to be arriving at your Sussex home in a matter of days. Sooner, perhaps. Hartley felt certain you would not require an explanation of what they were told."

Mr. Bentford paled immediately. Whatever the Duke of Hartley referred to in regard to Mr. Bentford's finances was indeed ruinous, and Mr. Bentford had easily ascertained the details though they had not been disclosed.

"There are several well-substantiated rumors spreading through Town," the duke further informed him. "Rumors which have already quite ruined any good standing you may have enjoyed there. I would not suggest returning."

Mr. Bentford's pallor increased, as did the avid stares he received. Clara fumbled for Corbin's hand. An almost painful thudding in her heart had begun. It was equal parts uncertainty and hope. His fingers threaded through hers as he silently watched the exchange in front of them.

"And I have my own message for you." The duke stepped closer to Mr. Bentford.

His Grace's gaze was so icy Clara felt the effect of it though it was directed at someone else. She stepped involuntarily backward. A small hand clutched hers. Clara looked down to find Edmund watching the duke in apprehensive awe. She glanced quickly at Alice, sleeping still. Corbin's eyes darted in her direction, holding hers for a moment before looking back at the Duke of Kielder, whose glare had now brought complete silence to the entranced crowd.

"I do not, nor will I ever, tolerate a man—notice I do not refer to you as a *gentleman*—who would mistreat a good and honest lady in the way I know you have." His jaw visibly tightened.

The entire crowd must have heard Mr. Bentford's swallow.

"Know this: while the Jonquils may have qualms about throwing a lying blackguard from an upper-story window or locking him in a swinging gibbet, *I* am the Duke of Kielder—I have no such pangs of conscience."

Mr. Bentford nodded frantically.

"I suggest you remove your dishonorable carcass from these hallowed grounds and hie yourself home to salvage what remains of your existence." The duke stepped back once more, looking for all the world as if he were having a discussion about the weather over tea. "And if you so much as send a letter to the lady you have been harassing, I assure you I will make good on my threats, both those I have voiced and those I will formulate when I am most angry with you."

There was no response, verbal or otherwise, only the sight of Mr. Bentford scurrying from the churchyard. Clara was certain she heard the duke mutter "coward" under his breath.

Corbin slipped his hand from hers. "I will return directly," he said and moved in the direction of the duke.

Clara closed her eyes, hardly daring to breathe a sigh of relief. Mr. Bentford might actually leave. Based on his reaction to the Duke of Kielder, he wasn't likely to harass her again. It was too much to believe.

"He is a little scary," Clara heard Edmund say. She looked down at him and saw his eyes glued to the Duke of Kielder.

"Yes, a little," Clara agreed. "But I do not think we need to fear him."

Edmund shook his head. "Corbin would have told us."

Clara smiled. "He most certainly would have." She turned her gaze to Corbin, who stood with the duke and those members of the Jonquil family who remained in the neighborhood. Alice slept soundly against his chest, no doubt drooling again.

"And he would keep us safe," Edmund added.

"Yes, he would." The Duke of Kielder may have delivered the ultimately effective threat, but Corbin was the one who made Clara feel safe and secure.

Corbin turned at that moment and looked directly at her, smiling. Clara's heart leaped into her throat. As he approached, she felt a shiver spread through her entire body, and all of her thoughts seemed to dissipate into oblivion. All but one. She loved this man. She loved him entirely.

"His Grace will be . . . will be taking his midday meal at Havenworth before returning to Town." Corbin smiled at Edmund as well and reached out to ruffle his hair. "Though he did find Alice's lack of enthusiasm for his visit rather lowering."

Clara laughed, and Corbin chuckled. Alice was sound asleep.

"Shall we?" Corbin held his free arm out to her.

Clara placed her arm through his and felt her heart swelling inside her. They stepped inside Corbin's carriage as they'd been doing each Sunday of late. Alice slept against his chest, a sight Clara hadn't yet grown tired of. How alone they'd all been for so long. But not any longer.

"Is Mr. Bentford really gone?" Edmund asked.

Corbin nodded firmly and confidently. "He is gone, and I am absolutely certain he will never come back."

Edmund's shoulders rose and fell with a deep breath. Clara could actually see the weight lifted from him.

She caught Corbin's gaze. "You did this for us," she said, awe filling her at the realization.

"Yes," he answered. "For *us*."

She sat silently at his side as they drove to Havenworth. Her mind couldn't seem to grasp the reality of her newfound freedom. She didn't have to run or hide any longer. Corbin, her Corbin, had done the impossible. He had given her peace.

Chapter Twenty-Five

CRISPIN APPROACHED CORBIN AFTER LUNCHEON, something he didn't often do. Philip and Layton were Crispin's particular friends, and he generally turned to them when he had a task or a question or a favor to ask.

"I have brought more with me from London than a mere duke. I have a message to deliver," Crispin said, a look of mischief and determination in his eyes. "While I personally am looking forward to delivering it, I thought you might appreciate being there too. You have an iron in this fire."

"What—?"

Crispin understood as well as any of Corbin's brothers the necessity of mentally finishing sentences at times. "I have a letter of particular importance for Finley, whom we both know is lingering about the area."

"Promise the letter brings bad news, and I'll deliver it myself."

"That it does, indeed." Crispin slapped Corbin on the shoulder before continuing. "Our good friend Finley will be on a mad dash for Town within the hour, I daresay."

Corbin needed no more encouragement than that. "I've an entire afternoon. Let's . . . let's find him."

They headed out to the stables. They had very nearly reached the paddock when an odd sound stopped Corbin. He thought he heard a horse, but *behind* the stables, not within them. The stable hands were thorough and reliable. He couldn't imagine any of them neglecting their duties.

He walked around the side of the long building, just to be certain none of the animals had wandered off. For just a moment, he couldn't entirely make sense of what he saw.

It was indeed a horse—Buttercup, in fact—with a saddle on her back. But the saddle was on backward. *Backward?* And next to Buttercup was Charlie, looking as though he meant to climb into the backward saddle and ride Buttercup facing the wrong direction.

Good heavens. "Charlie." The single word snapped out with exasperation and weariness.

Charlie looked over immediately. "Just going for a ride, Corbin."

His nearly perfected look of innocence didn't fool Corbin for a minute. Corbin whistled to Buttercup. She obeyed without hesitation, walking to where he stood. He took her rein, gave Charlie a lingering look of reprimand, then led the mare back to the stables.

Jim looked up from his work as Corbin passed with the missaddled mare. "What the blazes?"

"Have her unsaddled," Corbin instructed. "And see to it she has a quiet rest of the day."

Jim nodded, taking the rein from Corbin. "I would never have let yer brother take the poor creature if I'd've known he was up to this kind of tomfoolery."

Tomfoolery and Charlie were rather constant companions, it seemed.

Corbin sent one of the stable hands for his and Crispin's horses, then returned to the paddock.

"Seventeen isn't the most intelligent age," Crispin observed. "One can only hope Charlie outgrows it."

"Outgrows it before . . . before Mater really does strangle him."

They mounted their own horses and set out on their original errand. Crispin looked to Corbin, silently allowing him to choose the direction they took their search. He gave it a moment's thought. Finley had been present for Mr. Bentford's dismissal. He would know Clara's immediate concerns were settled. She, along with Catherine, had been Finley's focus the past weeks. Catherine, however, was in London.

"Ivy Cottage," Corbin said. "I've a feeling he'll be waiting for . . . looking for Clara."

Crispin nodded solemnly. "He never did know when to leave well enough alone."

Sure enough, Finley's mount was standing outside the cottage, its reins wrapped around the low-hanging branch of an obliging tree.

"The man is like a fox circling a henhouse," Crispin muttered.

Corbin looked across at him. "Sounds to me like it is fox hunting season."

Crispin's lips slowly turned up in a devilish smile. They walked to the front door. Corbin was relieved to find it locked. But where, then, was Finley?

"We should check around back," Crispin said. "He's probably looking for a loose window or a mouse hole to crawl in through."

They walked around the cottage and, sure enough, found Finley sniffing around the place.

"What have we here?" Crispin asked, his tone slow and menacing. "I do believe we've stumbled upon an intruder."

Finley met their gazes without the slightest hint of guilt. He always had been too sure of himself. His confidence had long ago jumped to arrogance. "Well, now. If it isn't the Jonquils come to champion the widows and orphans of the world," Finley drawled.

"Nothing of the sort, I assure you." Crispin reached into his jacket pocket. "I have a letter for you, one I'm told you will wish to receive with all possible haste."

The first hints of wariness entered Finley's expression.

Crispin held the letter in his hand but made no movement to give it to Finley. He simply slapped it back and forth against his other hand, watching Finley with unflagging calm.

Impatience slid across Finley's face. "Are you planning to simply stand there, or are you going to give me my letter?"

"We have two other things for you first," Crispin said.

Finley's gaze narrowed. He took a single, purposeful step toward them. "What is it?"

Crispin looked as cool and collected as ever. "You imposed upon my wife. You laid your grubby, filthy hands on her."

Finley raised a single eyebrow.

"If I hear at any point from this moment on that you have so much as spoken to her, I will expect you to name your seconds and your preferred gravedigger. Am I understood?"

Finley didn't nod, didn't flinch. But some of his arrogance dissipated. "You said you had *two* things."

"Indeed," Crispin said. "I have delivered mine. The second is for Corbin to deliver."

That was clear enough. Crispin had defended his wife with words. Corbin was no orator, but he meant to see to it Clara was clear of her last remaining tormentor.

He moved with determined footsteps to Finley, watching with satisfaction the nervousness the man couldn't quite hide.

"She's not your wife or family member," Finley objected. "Her honor is not yours to defend."

Corbin took hold of Finley's cravat and twisted it in his fist enough to make Finley's eyes bulge the slightest bit. He stepped in close, eye to eye with the scoundrel.

"I've broken one man's nose recently," he said. "I'll happily make it two."

Though Finley said nothing, Corbin saw the threat sink in. He released the cravat but lingered a moment, letting his glare have maximum impact. Finley took the smallest step backward.

Crispin was there in the next moment. He handed Finley the letter. "I was instructed to make certain you open it."

Finley broke the seal, though he clearly would have preferred not to. His eyes quickly darted back and forth across the page. Corbin actually saw him pale. Without a word, Finley pushed his way between them and rushed toward the front of the house.

"That did the trick," Crispin said with palpable satisfaction.

"What was in the letter?"

Crispin shrugged as his smile grew more amused. "A warning. Word has reached the various gentlemen's clubs that Finley has been harassing the wives and daughters of quite a few gentlemen, rumors that, no doubt, are being confirmed by his many victims. His only real options are to rush to Town and attempt to squelch the whispers or go into hiding somewhere out of reach of the many, many gentlemen who are even now calling for his head."

A corner of Corbin's mouth twitched upward. There was a poetic satisfaction in that. He would be forced by his own misdeeds to leave Clara, and every other woman, alone. Clara would be safe from him.

She was no longer living under a cloud of uncertainty or fear. She didn't have to leave. Didn't have to run any longer.

Corbin simply had to find a way to ask her to stay, not merely in the neighborhood but with him.

Chapter Twenty-Six

"I understand Mr. Finley has gone to Town," Mater said not long after the gentlemen joined the ladies after dinner that evening.

The Duke of Kielder and Crispin had headed back to London immediately after Corbin and Crispin had returned from Ivy Cottage.

"I believe he has, Mater," Layton answered. "Hopefully for some time."

"It seems the neighborhood will be emptying these next few days," Mater said. "Layton and Marion, and, of course, Caroline, will be returning to the Meadows. I must confess myself anxious to return to the Park. The remodel of the dower house must be nearly completed by now. I should very much like to see how it turned out."

Corbin let the conversation roll over him, not really hearing any of it. His mind was far too full of Clara. She hadn't come down to dinner. Was she still upset? Had she accidentally slept through the meal?

He stepped aside with Marion. "Do you know why . . . Where Clara is?"

She looked momentarily confused. "She returned to Ivy Cottage this afternoon. I thought you knew."

Returned to Ivy Cottage? Why would she do that? She hadn't left so much as a word of farewell. "And the children?" he pressed.

"The children as well."

What had gone wrong? He'd spent the past few days trying not to worry that he stumbled over his words, that he was uneasy in company, that he hadn't the polish or poise of his brothers. He'd told himself that she wouldn't mind that he would never be a man of influence or greatness. He'd simply been Corbin Jonquil in a way he hadn't been for anyone in years. For all that, she hadn't stayed with him. She'd left him.

"Corbin?" Layton's voice, quiet and urgent, broke into his thoughts.

The last thing Corbin wanted was pity, or worse, more brotherly advice. What good had any of his brothers' advice done him? "There is a foal . . . a foal in the stables that isn't . . . hasn't—" He left it at that and made his way from the room.

He didn't stop until he'd reached the stables. If anyone was surprised to see him, they didn't let on. Corbin offered a quick nod where it was called for and made his way to the back. Whipster seemed no more surprised than any of the others.

"Hey, boy," Corbin greeted him, rubbing his nose. "Can I come sit with you?"

The horse nickered, nudging Corbin with his nose. Corbin stepped into the stall and, taking a brush from the wall, began rhythmically grooming. Being with Whipster always made Corbin feel closer to Father.

There were a lot of things he had wished over the past ten years that he could have asked his father. He felt that need keenly just now. *What did I do wrong? What is it about me she doesn't like?* He silently thought through his dilemma as he brushed. Eventually, he finished his ministrations but didn't feel any closer to the answers he needed.

Corbin sat on the bench he'd kept at the back of Whipster's stall for years. He'd been coming to this spot ever since he'd arrived at Havenworth. He came there when he was frustrated, upset, confused, lonely.

Why haven't I sat here lately? Corbin wondered silently. The past weeks had certainly been confusing, frustrating, and upsetting at times. What was different tonight from a fortnight before?

He knew the answer almost before the question had formed in his mind. He was lonely. The past weeks he'd had some hope that Clara would remain, that she would return his love. That had kept the loneliness at bay.

Well, Father, Corbin silently said, Whipster bumping him with his nose, his neck bent down to him, *what do I do now?* Corbin reached up and rubbed Whipster's nose in acknowledgment of his attention. *I've done all I know how.*

"Is that old Whipster?"

Corbin looked up at the sound of Layton's voice. He nodded.

Layton leaned against the stall door. He didn't say anything, just watched Whipster, his expression unreadable. Then after a moment, he said, "Do you remember, Corbin, when Philip said he wouldn't ride with you because Whipster was the stupidest horse he'd ever seen?"

Corbin nodded, letting his eyes settle back on Whipster. Philip had said that about three months after Father had given the colt to Corbin.

Corbin been hurt by the comment, probably more than Philip had realized. If Whipster was a stupid horse, Corbin had thought at the time, it was probably because he had done something wrong in caring for him.

"And Father told us that the puppy Philip had decided to take as his own from Golden Girl's litter had taken ill and died only the day before," Layton went on. Corbin remembered. "Father said people often say or do things when they are hurting that they wouldn't say or do otherwise. He said Philip needed time to recover from his loss and that we needed to be patient with him."

Father had explained that. Corbin remembered feeling deeply relieved when Father had assured him there was nothing the matter with Whipster, that Philip needed to work through his grief and loss.

"From what I have heard," Layton continued, "you have had more advice from us brothers than any man should have to endure." There was a chuckle in his voice that didn't take away from his sincerity. Corbin looked up at him again. Layton offered an almost-sad smile, the kind he'd worn with regularity before Marion had come into his life. "I thought perhaps you needed some wisdom from Father instead."

Corbin wasn't sure how long he sat in the stall after Layton walked away.

Time to recover. Layton referred to Clara, then? It seemed so. All the other bits of advice he'd received were in regard to her.

Philip had insulted Whipster because he was hurting. Clara, perhaps, had left for similar reasons. And, like Philip, maybe she needed time and space to settle her thoughts.

Could he give her that? Could he step away and let her make up her mind? He wanted her to choose him, and if she did, he wanted it to be because she loved him, not because she felt pressured. That, it seemed, meant letting her slip out of his life.

But only temporarily. Just until she recovered from the difficulties of the past days and months and years.

He could do that. He told himself several times that he could. If Clara needed time and patience and space, he could give her that. He would.

Corbin let out a deep breath, hoping he wasn't wrong in this path he was choosing.

Chapter Twenty-Seven

Spring brought a rainbow of wildflowers to the meadow surrounding Ivy Cottage. Clara spent her afternoons watching Edmund after he returned each day from the Havenworth stables and Alice running and playing in the meadow. She watched them, often joined in their games, but inside, her heart was aching.

She'd brought the children back to Ivy Cottage the day the Duke of Kielder sent Mr. Bentford running for the hills. Alice and Edmund had been upended and overwhelmed. She'd hoped to give them a little quiet time, a chance to calm their worries.

She'd allowed herself to hope Corbin would come see her. Mr. Finley had insisted she was nothing more to Corbin or his family than the latest Jonquil charitable endeavor. In her heart, she had truly believed Corbin loved her.

But more than a week had passed, and he hadn't come. He sat behind them at church, but he rode his own horse home afterward, leaving his carriage behind to take them home. He didn't visit, didn't send any word or greeting home with Edmund day after day.

In the first days after Mr. Bentford's machinations had been thwarted, she'd written letters of gratitude to all those who had played a role in that miracle. But she couldn't bring herself to write to Corbin. Anything she might have penned would have fallen far short of what she felt.

For the children's sake, she kept a smile on her face and tried to focus on all the reasons she had for rejoicing. Mr. Bentford was out of their lives. She'd received her quarterly payment at last, so they had money to live on. Mr. Finley hadn't been seen in the neighborhood since the day of the Duke of Kielder's visit. She focused on that and did her utmost to keep all other thoughts out of her mind.

She tucked the children into bed each night. That undertaking was one of the highlights of her day. Until they asked difficult questions.

"Mama," Alice said from beneath her quilt that night. "Where is Mister?"

Clara kept her expression light, though the question pierced her soul. "He is busy with his horses, dear. But you saw him at church on Sunday. He played peekaboo with you."

She pouted. "Where is Mister?"

"He is probably asleep, Alice. It is sleeping time."

Her little brow wrinkled in thought. "Mister is sleeping?"

Clara nodded slowly and pointedly. Alice's eyes opened wide. She nodded too. In a movement so swift Clara didn't believe it for a moment, Alice tipped her head to the side and shut her eyes as if very suddenly asleep herself. Clara kissed her cheek and smoothed the quilt.

"Good night, Alice," she whispered and walked to the bedroom door. She glanced back at her sweet angel.

Even absent from their lives, Corbin was a blessing. The mere suggestion that he was doing something was enough to convince Alice to do it as well. Alice loved him so deeply. Eventually, she would realize her beloved Mister was not coming back, and her tiny heart would shatter.

Clara blinked back a sudden sheen of tears and took a breath to calm herself. Somehow she would hold this family together.

She stepped into Edmund's room next. He was sitting on a chair at his window, glancing out into the dark night.

"Time for bed, Edmund."

He didn't look back at her. "I can see the lights at Havenworth from here," he said.

"I have noticed them myself."

"Corbin is visiting his family," Edmund said. "It's lonely at the stables without him."

"Visiting his family?" She hadn't heard Corbin was gone. Perhaps that was the reason she hadn't seen him. "How long ago did he leave?"

"Yesterday."

Then his journey wasn't the reason for his absence in the days before that. Clara pushed down her disappointment.

She stopped at the window, settling her arm around Edmund's shoulder. "You miss him," she said.

"You don't think he'll forget about me, do you?" Poor Edmund sounded so worried, so lonely.

She squeezed his shoulders. "He won't. And I am absolutely certain he misses you as well."

"I thought he was going to come here and say farewell before he left," Edmund said. "Why didn't he?"

Clara swallowed against the emotion surfacing once more. "He probably meant to but ran too short on time."

"Probably." How she hoped Edmund would be satisfied with that. She couldn't bear examining her own loneliness in any greater depth.

"Come on over to your bed, sweetheart."

He came without argument, though his gaze returned to his window even after he lay down. He missed Corbin. Alice missed Corbin. Clara's heart broke with missing him.

She gave Edmund the same kiss on the cheek she gave both children every night, then returned to her own room with a heavy heart. She sat on the edge of her bed, telling herself to simply breathe through her pain. Life hadn't crushed her before, and she wouldn't allow it to now.

* * *

Philip and Sorrel returned from Scotland to Lampton Park. Corbin made the trip to see them, grateful for an excuse to get away. Sorrel could walk a few steps without her walking stick and, according to Philip, was improving daily. She still appeared to be in some pain, but Philip insisted that was to be expected, since her hip could never be restored.

There was an apothecary in Northumberland, Philip said, who had developed a brace for rheumatic hips that Dr. MacAslon had some hope might relieve a little of Sorrel's difficulties on that score. Sorrel herself said little, though her continued pallor spoke volumes. She was improving but slowly.

Charlie remained at the Park and, according to Mater and Philip, kept up his tradition of getting into scrapes. Layton, Marion, and Caroline were in Town. Jason was too, as always. Harold made the occasional appearance during Corbin's week-long stay but always had something of monumental importance to see to.

Everyone was busy or gone, and Corbin quickly found himself anxious to return home. Edmund would miss him, if no one else. And there hadn't been a single brown-haired little girl to play peekaboo with during church or an emerald-eyed beauty to watch from a distance. And he lived for the brief glimpses he had of Clara. Sweet, beautiful, loving Clara.

Only a few times had his family brought her up. Corbin had managed to shrug off their inquiries. After a time, they'd stopped asking. Mater, however, had watched him very closely, a look of sadness and disappointment in her eyes. That look alone had convinced him the time had come to return to Havenworth.

Somehow, before his departure, Charlie had been added to the traveling party. "Just keep him busy," Philip pleaded dramatically. "He'll be at Cambridge in another month. If you can keep him out of trouble until then, I will be eternally grateful."

Corbin nodded.

"And Mater needs some peace," Philip added, his expression suddenly more serious.

"Is something wrong with Mater?"

Philip shook his head. "Napoleon is coming nearer Brussels with each passing day."

"Stanley," Corbin answered with a whisper. Stanley's regiment was in Brussels, along with the rest of the Coalition forces.

Philip nodded. "The latest dispatches from Wellington warn our leaders to prepare themselves for a battle unlike any Britain has ever fought."

"It is likely to . . . to be—"

"If predictions prove correct, the coming conflict will be extremely deadly," Philip confirmed.

Corbin nodded once more. "You'll take care of Mater?"

"Of course." Philip smiled back at him. "And I'm certain Holy Harry will pray, so we should be fine."

"Send word when you . . . when Charlie needs to return."

Philip nodded. "Thanks, Cor."

Corbin smiled at that. His brothers hadn't called him Cor since he was eight years old.

"C'mon, Charlie," Corbin said to his youngest brother, who actually looked relatively happy to be accompanying him back to Havenworth.

During the ride back, Corbin thought over the past months. Clara's arrival in the neighborhood. Philip and Layton's weddings. Stanley's leaving for the Continent and the continued warfare. Trying to win Clara's heart. Gaining two children he would always think of as his own.

He'd spent a long and lonely week at Havenworth after Clara's departure and another week at Lampton Park after that. He still loved her. That hadn't changed. He doubted it ever would. She was good and kind and loving. She was beautiful and graceful. He missed her. Did she miss him?

Had he given her the space she needed? Was she still sorting things out?

He didn't know. But he was continuing to live his life the best he could without her there. He was closer to his brothers than he'd ever been before. He enjoyed Edmund and Alice, though from more of a distance than he preferred. And he felt more content than he remembered feeling in years. He would never be his brothers' equal in society or be comfortable in crowds or in front of people, but he had a home he'd grown to love every bit as much as his childhood home, neighbors he cared about, a successful business, and family nearby.

And if there was even the slightest bit of fairness in the world, Clara would come back to him.

Chapter Twenty-Eight

Clara slipped into the copse of trees and the welcome shade offered there. A few more yards to the east and she would be on Havenworth land. Corbin wouldn't object; she knew that instinctively. He was too much of a gentleman and too good a neighbor to do so.

"Oh, Corbin," she whispered as she walked. She had convinced herself in the first few months after coming to Ivy Cottage that she would never let another man into her life again. Until she'd met Corbin, it had been true. Having known him, having felt the joy of a good man at her side, having felt love, she knew now she would always regret what she might have had.

Part of her still hoped, despite his prolonged absence, that he did care for her. She thought back on the one kiss they'd shared and found she couldn't entirely dismiss it as friendly or pitying. She was a coward, and she knew it. If only she had the courage to simply go ask him if he loved her.

Movement not far distant caught Clara's eye. She looked warily in that direction. Tall, lean, and golden-haired—whoever it was had to be a Jonquil. She knew, despite not seeing the person at all clearly, it was not Corbin. Edmund had told her the day before that Charlie, the youngest of the seven brothers, had come to Havenworth to stay for a while.

Clara smiled, wondering what mischief Charlie had gotten himself into. That was, she felt certain, the reason for his banishment from Lampton Park. She liked Charlie and had a feeling it was not a mischievous nature that was his undoing but youth and undirected energy. Time in the stables would do him good.

She had intended to avoid him, but Charlie caught sight of her. He joined her approximately where the property line ran.

"Good day, Mrs. Bentford," he said with an appropriate bow. Clara could see in that gesture that he would be very much like his brothers when he was fully grown: genteel, well mannered, and kind. He would probably break a whole string of hearts.

"Good day to you, Mr. Jonquil."

Charlie winced at the name.

Clara laughed lightly as they began walking again. "If you are to be a Cambridge man soon, you must grow accustomed to being addressed formally and as an adult."

"I know." He sighed with a smile. "But there are a lot of *Mr. Jonquils*."

"You all are very much alike," Clara acknowledged. "And yet, as far as I was able to observe, you are also quite different from one another."

"Yes," Charlie answered, though there was the tiniest hint of bitterness in his voice. Clara wondered at it. "The earl who cuts a dash through Town. The widower who has found love again. The most successful horse breeder in the midlands. The famously successful barrister. The youngest in the Dragoons to reach the rank of captain. The top-of-his-class vicar. And Charlie."

So that was part of the problem—he hadn't yet found his place in the world or in his family. "Have you thought about what you would like to study when you reach Cambridge?"

Charlie shrugged. "What's left?"

"Have you spoken with any of your brothers about this? I imagine they might have some advice for you."

"They're busy," Charlie answered.

They walked for a time in silence. Clara wished she could do more for Charlie. She knew how it felt to be lost and wandering without direction. She'd felt that way in the short interval between the announcement of her betrothal to Mr. Bentford and their wedding. She'd felt that way between Mr. Bentford's death and his brother's arrival at Bentford Manor. She'd felt that way the past weeks without Corbin.

"So why do you never come to Havenworth anymore?" Charlie asked after a moment.

Clara was too caught off guard to do anything but stare at him. Why did she never come to Havenworth? What made Charlie think she was expected there?

"Corbin's miserable, you know," Charlie said, shoving his hands in his pockets.

"Miserable?"

"He tries not to be." Charlie shrugged. Then he laughed a little. "I don't think any of us thought he'd ever talk to a lady enough to actually fall in love with her."

"Fall—?" That was all she got out.

"Guess even the Jonquils can be wrong."

In love? Corbin is in love with me? Enough that he misses me when I'm gone? Misses me to the point of misery? The realization struck her with unexpected force. No one had ever mourned her absence or wanted her in his life enough to miss her. She stopped on the spot, her thoughts spinning. "Are you certain?"

"That Jonquils can be wrong?" Charlie asked, genuinely surprised.

"That Corbin is in love with—"

"You," he finished for her and nodded. Then his mouth dropped open in sudden understanding. "Ah, Lud. I probably wasn't supposed to tell you that."

Clara focused on Charlie. "Do you really think so?"

Charlie nodded, looking evermore uncomfortable. "It's rather obvious." He spoke almost apologetically.

Suddenly, Clara found her courage returning with force. "Thank you, Charlie," she said, moving quickly in the direction of Havenworth. "Thank you."

* * *

"I think that's good for now, Edmund," Corbin said. Johnny stayed nearby as Edmund rode Happy Helper to the side of the paddock. The boy was riding better every day. "Dismount and take him to his stall. Don't forget to brush him thoroughly."

Edmund smiled and nodded.

"I'll come check in a few minutes," Corbin added.

If Edmund was surprised that Corbin wasn't following him, he didn't let it show. Corbin waited until Edmund, with Johnny's supervision, led Happy Helper from the paddock. He turned quickly and walked out toward the back grounds of Havenworth. He needed a few minutes' respite.

Edmund had done so many things that afternoon that reminded Corbin of Clara: expressions on his face, phrases that belonged to her. It had been acutely torturous.

He'd take a few minutes to clear his head.

"Corbin!"

Now he was hearing things. He'd imagined Clara's voice saying his name over the past few weeks. It had simply never been so realistic.

"Corbin!"

Twice in a row seemed very unlikely. Corbin turned toward the sound, and his heart stopped. Clara. Hurrying toward him. His first fleeting feeling was that she'd come back to him. Then he realized she looked distressed.

Something had happened. Gracious heavens! Alice? Was Alice ill? Or hurt? Was Clara unwell?

Corbin didn't hesitate a moment longer. He ran to meet her partway. Without a word, Clara threw her arms around his neck and buried her head against his shoulder. Corbin wrapped his arms protectively around her.

"What is it, Clara?" he asked, alarmed. "Has something happened? Is . . . Is someone ill or . . . or injured?"

"Oh, Corbin!"

"What is it?" Corbin pulled her away from him enough to study her. "Tell me, Clara. Please."

"I saw Charlie when I was walking—"

Something had happened to Charlie. From the look on Clara's face, something drastic. Taking hold of her hand, Corbin instantly headed in the direction she'd come.

"Corbin." Clara tugged at his hand.

"Was he . . . was he hurt?"

"No, Corbin." She tugged again. They were at the edge of the trees. "Charlie was quite well."

"Then what has you so distressed?" Corbin turned back to her. "You cannot tell me you aren't. I can see it on your face."

"Not distressed," she insisted, her eyes never wavering from his. There was a nervousness, an anxious anticipation there that Corbin could not possibly interpret.

"But you're upset." He touched her face as he spoke. "Did Charlie upset you? Did he . . . did he say something—"

Clara shook her head. "Nothing unkind."

That was a very good thing for Charlie. Corbin would not have tolerated any unkindness toward Clara. And yet, she was still teary. She was almost never teary.

Corbin instinctively reached up and ran a soothing finger across the worry lines that creased her forehead. She closed her eyes and seemed to sigh, as if his gesture had relieved some of her tension.

"I have to know, Corbin. The not knowing is killing me."

"Know what?" He caressed her cheek with his hand. She leaned into his hand.

"Charlie told me that you love me," Clara whispered.

Corbin froze. A kick in the gut from Devil's Advocate certainly couldn't have caught him more by surprise. He couldn't formulate a response, could barely register what she'd said, even as it repeated in his brain. *He told me that you love me.*

She opened her eyes and looked up at him. "Do you?" she asked, her voice even quieter than it had been and far more uncertain.

Corbin swallowed. *With all my heart. Absolutely. Forever.* No words escaped his mouth.

A look of pain crossed her features, and she stepped back, away from him. "Why not?" Then, as if suddenly realizing she'd uttered the pain-ridden question out loud, Clara clamped her mouth shut and stepped back farther. She shook her head. "Please, don't answer that."

Corbin hadn't seen such a look of anguish on her face. Even Mr. Bentford's appearance hadn't brought such pain to her expressive eyes.

She thought he didn't love her.

Clara turned and began to walk quickly away from him. Before she'd even taken two steps, Corbin took hold of her arm. He turned her gently to face him. She was weeping.

"Oh, Clara," he said.

She seemed to crumple right there in front of him. Corbin wrapped his arms around her and pulled her to him. Each breath she took shuddered.

"Clara." He breathed her name, his face directly beside hers. "I . . . I don't say things—" Corbin stopped and took a breath, trying to force his thoughts into some semblance of order. "Clara. I do love . . . I have loved you from the first time I met you." He had dropped to the level of a whisper by the time the final admission came out.

He felt her shift against him and watched as she turned her face up toward him. Even shining with tears, her green eyes were spectacular.

"You truly do?"

"Truly."

Corbin kissed her tenderly on the forehead. "I have missed you, Clara," he whispered. "Every minute since you left."

"But you never came."

"I didn't think you wanted me to."

"Oh, Corbin." She sighed, leaning against him. "I have been miserable without you. I love you, Corbin. I love you too much to live without you any longer."

He closed his eyes and let those words settle over him. She loved him. Clara, *his* Clara, whom he had loved in silence from almost the first moment he'd seen her, loved him.

He felt her slender fingers gently touch his jaw near his ear. "Corbin?" she asked, coaxing his eyes open once more. She was watching him closely.

"I have misunderstood you, misjudged you. So many times, Corbin. I thought you disliked me or thought yourself above me or—" Clara's color deepened with each sentence. "I never dreamed I would find a gentleman who was kind and gentle and everything I always dreamed of but never thought I would find."

He was what she'd wished for? Corbin kept Clara in his arms, pulled up close to him. "You don't mind that . . . that I—" He stopped for a breath and to order his thoughts. "I don't express myself well. I will never be as well known as my brothers. Or as commanding or fashionable or—"

"I love you, Corbin," she said, looking intently into his eyes. "Just as you are. Precisely as you are."

He held her ever tighter. Her cheeks were rosy, her eyes bright, her lips smiling.

My Clara. The thought repeated in his mind. *My Clara.*

He shifted one hand to her face and lowered his head until their lips met. Their first kiss had been a nerve-racking experiment in intuition. While Corbin hardly felt himself skilled in the art of kissing, there was not the uncertainty he'd felt before. He gently pressed his lips to hers, then more fervently, feeling, in a way, that his mouth was finally communicating what he never seemed able to make it say.

"Clara," he whispered when their mouths parted, though he remained a hair's breadth away. "My Clara."

"I love you," she whispered in reply.

"I love you," he answered, and he kissed her again.

They, of course, would tell the children, would send word to Lampton Park. But that moment, that one moment, was theirs.

Chapter Twenty-Nine

Corbin leaned against the doorframe of his library, his smile firmly in place. Edmund sat on the floor near the fireplace, drawing with a charcoal pencil on a piece of parchment. Alice was near him, spinning in a circle, her tiny hand firmly gripping the doll Corbin had given her a fortnight earlier, on the day she had become his stepdaughter.

He'd gone from being a bachelor, alone and lonely, to having an instant, beloved family. The children had made the transition from Ivy Cottage to Havenworth smoothly and cheerfully. Most important of all, Clara seemed genuinely content.

Alice abruptly finished her spinning game. She stumbled around a bit, eyes wide and still turning about in her head. Corbin held back a chuckle. She made a very indirect path to Edmund and stood a moment, her dizziness slowly decreasing.

Edmund glanced up at her but returned his gaze almost immediately to his papers.

Alice held her doll up on level with Edmund's downturned face. "Dolly kisses," she said.

A look of alarm passed over Edmund's face. "I don't want any dolly kisses," he insisted.

"Give dolly kisses!" With that declaration, Alice went about making a very valiant attempt to force her doll upon the poor boy.

Edmund's efforts to thwart her did not prove the deterrent he likely thought they would be. Alice climbed over and on him, pressing her doll's face against him wherever she could reach. Edmund was summarily kissed on the shoulder, arm, face, and hair. Alice's continued command for dolly kisses melded with Edmund's pleas that she stop. The two children were soon laughing.

Corbin allowed his own chuckle to escape. Both pairs of eyes turned to him. Edmund reached his side first.

"She is making her doll kiss me," Edmund told him, his tone both that of a much-put-upon young man and an amused older brother.

Sure enough, Alice ran toward them both, her doll held out threateningly as she giggled. "Dolly kisses for Mister!"

"I am done for, Edmund." Corbin made the observation quite dramatically, earning a grin from the boy. "Look after the horses, and tell your aunt Clara I . . . I was brave right to the end."

Edmund nodded seriously but with an amused twinkle in his eyes.

Corbin scooped Alice up. When she accosted him in the same way she had Edmund, he pretended to be desperate to escape, though he held her to him lovingly. With her in his arms and Edmund trailing after them, Corbin danced her about the room. Alice forgot entirely about her kissing game and simply wrapped her arms around his neck, squealing in delight when he spun.

After several minutes, their game left Corbin more than a little dizzy but chuckling right along with the children. He dropped onto the sofa, lying against one arm. Alice curled up on his chest. Edmund sat on the sofa's far arm.

"Mister tired?"

"Yes, love. Mister is tired."

She patted his cheek. "G'night, Mister."

Corbin closed his eyes, playing along with her latest game. The room grew quiet and still. After a moment, he felt an arm, small but too long to be Alice's, laid across him. He opened one eye a sliver and saw that Edmund had come to kneel beside the sofa. He rested his head against Corbin's chest near where Alice lay, with one arm draped over Corbin in something of an embrace.

He closed his eyes once more. A feeling of peace like he'd never known before had settled over him and the house since Clara and the children had come to live there.

"Mister sleepy."

Would Alice always call him Mister? he wondered. Maybe someday she would come to think of him as Papa. Corbin gently stroked her hair without opening his eyes. "Very sleepy," he said. He allowed the briefest of moments to pass before producing an overly loud snore that set Alice to giggling. Thoroughly enjoying her reaction, he snored again.

"I happen to know that you do not snore."

When had Clara entered the room? He opened his eyes on the instant. She knelt beside Edmund, very near Corbin's head.

"I was . . . just—"

"Loving my children," she finished for him.

"*Our* children," he whispered back. Surely she knew he thought of them as his own.

She tenderly smiled at him before turning to look at the children. "Jenny is waiting to take you to the nursery to wash for dinner. Hurry along."

Edmund obeyed more swiftly than Alice. She took a moment to pat Corbin's cheek once more and say, "G'night, Mister."

As she scrambled off of him and made her way to the door, where the nursemaid, Jenny, stood waiting for her, Corbin shifted upright. Clara still knelt beside the sofa, her gaze once more on him.

His heart dropped. "There are tears in your eyes."

She shook her head. "It's nothing."

"No." He held out his hand to her. "Your tears aren't ever nothing."

She took his hand and allowed him to help her to her feet and willingly sat on the sofa beside him.

He held her hands in his. "What has upset you?"

"I am not upset, really. Merely contemplative."

He kept her hands in one of his, freeing the other to stroke her hair. He loved the silkiness of it, loved that he now had the right to that gesture of affection. "Are you . . . contemplating something . . . unpleasant, then?"

"The children are so happy." More moisture gathered in her eyes. "Only a year ago we were living in misery and fear. I cannot think back on that without—" Her voice broke.

"My Clara." Corbin took her face in his hands and pressed a kiss to her forehead, lingering over the caress. He hoped that time would someday lessen the pain of her past. He loved her too deeply to bear the pain he too often still saw in her eyes.

She leaned into his embrace, resting her head against his shoulder, her hands pressed to his chest. Corbin had discovered quickly how very much she needed the reassurance of being held, though at first she'd been reluctant to allow him to do so.

"You have said how . . . how happy the children are." He rubbed her back as she lay silently in his arms. "Are you happy, my Clara?"

From within the circle of his arms, she answered quietly. "I used to think good men did not exist. But then I met you, Corbin Jonquil, and discovered I was wrong. All my life I kept hoping you were out there somewhere and that when I found you, you would love me."

"You were . . . hoping for a . . . stuttering, awkward . . . ?"

She pulled back from him enough to give him the glare with which he'd become very swiftly acquainted over the preceding fortnight. Corbin stopped his teasing protest and kept his smile firmly tucked away. He ought not rib her as he did, but her fierce defense of her bumbling husband never failed to touch him. He felt unspeakably blessed that the lady he loved returned his regard despite his lack of polish.

Clara's look remained severe. "You will not insult the man I've dreamed about all my life."

He held back a grin. "These dreams of yours sound like nightmare—"

Her fingertips pressed to his lips cut off his words. "Do not, Corbin." She slipped her fingers to his cheek. "You are wonderful, and I will not have anyone, including you, say otherwise."

"I am the man of your dreams?" He smiled a little at the thought.

"Of every"—she pressed a kiss to his lips—"single"—she kissed him again—"dream."

She'd so often seemed burdened and unhappy those months after she'd moved into the neighborhood. Her happiness had quickly become essential to him. She smiled more lately. The haunted look had left her eyes. Tension no longer pulled at her mouth or creased her forehead.

Corbin pulled her into his arms again. He kissed the top of her head, burying his face in her hair, breathing deep the fragrance she wore. "Will you promise . . . promise me something, Clara?"

"Anything at all."

"Promise you will tell me all of your dreams, my love."

She didn't pull out of his embrace. "My dreams?"

"I intend to make them come true." He kissed her forehead. "Every"—he shifted and kissed her cheek—"single"—he pressed a quick kiss to her lips—"dream."

"And if I told you that you already have?"

He smiled. "Then you shall simply have to dream up more."

"Perhaps we might think of some we could share," she said.

Having her there in his home, in his life, in his arms, there did not seem to be a dream that was out of his reach. All his life he'd felt like the outsider, overlooked and unimportant. Then he'd found his Clara, and he now knew where he belonged. She had learned to love him, quiet and unobtrusive, stuttering and lacking in polish—she had come to love him exactly as he was.

About the Author

SARAH M. EDEN READ HER first Jane Austen novel in elementary school and has been an Austen addict ever since. Fascinated by the English Regency era, Eden became a regular in that section of the reference department at her local library, where she painstakingly researched this extraordinary chapter in history. Eden is an award-winning author of short stories and was a Whitney Award finalist for her novels *Seeking Persephone* and *Courting Miss Lancaster*. Visit her at www.sarahmeden.com.